PRAISE FOR
Natives and Exotics

"Nadine Gordimer. Julian Barnes. Anita Brookner. Jane Alison. Jane Who? Alison, trust me, will join their company—elegant, cosmopolitan, enduring writers who make whatever they take on instantly absorbing—if the 43-year-old writer, a U.S. citizen born in Australia, raised in the United States, and now living in Germany, keeps this up . . . Is *Natives and Exotics* about colonialist imperialism through a child's eye? A veiled cry for sustainable environments? A counterhymn to Francis Bacon's dictate that man master nature? A love letter to Alison's family tree? *Natives and Exotics* touches all those themes. Sentence by sentence, Alison's eclectic sensibility, tuned ear, and camera eye sharpen the concretized aftereffects of, one guesses, her own prodigious travels."
—*The Philadelphia Inquirer*

"With luxurious prose and well-researched details, Alison stakes a powerful claim to the best socially conscious literature."
—*The Charlotte Observer*

"A kind of family album where, finally, no one is out of place."
—*The New York Times Book Review*

"All will savor the breathtaking imagery and philosophical wanderlust of *Natives and Exotics*."
—*The Times-Picayune* (New Orleans)

"A tender, lyrical novel that explores the consequences of so-called 'progress' . . . A lush evocation of the way people love and alter (and are altered by) the environments they inhabit."
—*Publishers Weekly*

"Intricate, ambitious, often beautiful."   —*Kirkus Reviews*

"Thought-provoking, and the language is spare and beautiful."
—*School Library Journal*

"More distinctive work from the author of *The Love-Artist*."
—*Library Journal*

Natives and Exotics

JANE ALISON

Natives and Exotics

A HARVEST BOOK
HARCOURT, INC.
Orlando   Austin   New York   San Diego   Toronto   London

www.HarcourtBooks.com

The Library of Congress has cataloged the hardcover edition as follows:
Alison, Jane.
Natives and exotics/Jane Alison.
p. cm.
1. Nature—Effect of human beings on—Fiction.
2. Scots—Foreign countries—Fiction.   3. Women pioneers—Fiction.
4. Human ecology—Fiction.   5. South America—Fiction.
6. Immigrants—Fiction.   7. Diplomats—Fiction.   8. Gardeners—Fiction.
9. Australia—Fiction.   10. Azores—Fiction.   I. Title.
PS3551.L366N38 2005
813'.6—dc22   2004023118
ISBN-13: 978-0-15-101201-5   ISBN-10: 0-15-101201-6
ISBN-13: 978-0-15-603247-6 (pbk.)   ISBN-10: 0-15-603247-3 (pbk.)

Text set in Adobe Caslon
Designed by Linda Lockowitz

Printed in the United States of America

First Harvest edition 2006
A C E G I K J H F D B

*In memory of
Edna, Sadie, and Arch*

CONTENTS

Natives and Exotics

Galápagos, 1786

ON THE BEACH of an island in the Pacific, an island with black sand, hardened black lava, and nothing green growing but cactus, a British mariner with a knife in his hand was crouching before a giant tortoise. The sailor was dirty and salty, but he wasn't hungry, and thanks to all the lime juice he'd drunk his gums weren't bleeding, his hair was still rooted, his breath wasn't as foul as it might be, and his lips were pinker than black. He was hale. So he didn't plan to kill the tortoise; he'd never been much good at that anyway. He had sailed the Pacific with the famous Captain Cook and seen the wonders of Tahiti, Terra Australis, all the rest. But now Cook was gone, killed by natives in the Sandwich Isles, and he himself had joined a whaler. Whaling didn't suit him, but he liked exploration, and now lo and behold he found himself on an island that looked like an upcropping of Hell.

"Still, now," the sailor whispered. He reached out cautiously to pat the animal and was surprised at how it felt. The tortoise raised its wormy head and fixed him with an old eye above its nostriled beak.

The waves broke behind them on the black sand, the equatorial sun burned overhead, and for a moment the two looked at each other. The tortoise's leathery legs—how ancient, the sailor thought. When in Creation had this monster been made? Yet its long, wrinkled neck was so like his own sorry gray member tucked away in his trousers that he grew embarrassed looking at it. And the way the skinny neck disappeared between the animal's breastplate and shell—a squirming, live thing slipping hidden into dead stony stuff— it seemed suddenly like the Mystery of Mysteries, the very source of Life . . .

But this sailor was not made to ponder such thoughts. Quickly he jumped on the tortoise's back. The animal didn't stir but received him, indignant.

So now? It was difficult to sit up there; the shell was bumpy, slippery. The mariner clasped the beast between his legs and spurred with his heels, but the tortoise wouldn't move; he spurred it again, but soon felt sheepish. He looked out at the glaring sea.

Well then, what else?

The shell took his knife well. It was better than meerschaum, much better than whale tooth. Holding the rim of the shell with one hand, with the other he carved: s. c. 1786.

So there he was. He looked at his work. A small gesture, but it cheered him, like slipping a message in a bottle, tossing it into the damnable sea, and God only knew who might find it. He himself would leave no more than a heap of bones on a beach somewhere, crumbling back into sand.

The sailor slid off the tortoise, and again the two looked at each other.

"That's that," he said. "So long!" He patted the animal on the shell, a little sorry to go.

The tortoise, released, lumbered off, over the hot volcanic sand.

London, 1786

IN SOHO SQUARE, Sir Joseph Banks was sitting at his desk, pondering a globe. He had a large bulldog head, wavy white hair, fierce eyes. Around him in the library were his natural collections, mementoes from when he'd sailed the *Endeavour* with Captain Cook: the small reddish kangaroo he'd hunted in Terra Australis, which now sat limp and stuffed on his shelf; the wandering albatross he'd shot from deck, its wings spanning nine feet; a polished Maori skull on a pedestal; and his prize: an etching of a tree with flowers like barnacles that was now called *Banksia grandis*. A new tree he himself had found. So gratifying to have one's name fixed on the world!

Since his adventures, Banks had been busy sending other men out to do as he had done, to discover and seize the world's living wealth. Because now that the last continent had been found and Britain ruled the waves, the possibilities were intoxicating. He presided over Kew Gardens and had a hand in all colonial affairs, and he sent eager young botanists to Australia, Africa, North and South America, to hunt new plants and ship them home to Kew. Plants of utility, plants of strange beauty. Banks inspected the wonders and decided what should go where in the world—because there was no reason to let things stay as they *were*, after all. Exploration preceded colonization, and colonization preceded trade, and that was the natural order of things. The world was open for rearrangement. As he pondered the globe, eyes skimming the continents and oceans, he polished his coup de grâce.

He drew his finger from England down and around to newfound Australis; then he drew an imaginary line from a small archipelago near that last continent to another cluster of islands in the west. Two elegant migrations of plants and souls. Britain would make empty Terra Australis a penal colony: his idea had finally won. But you could not ship only *men* there. *Indigo, coffee, cotton, tobacco, oranges, & lemons*, he wrote in a memorandum: that's what would accompany the convicts on the *Guardian*. Men, women, juveniles below deck, plants and little fruit trees in a greenhouse above. So in one stroke he would people and plant a new continent. How grand to work on this scale! *Genesis*.

And now the other migration; the symmetry so pleased him. *Breadfruit*, he wrote; *Bounty, Wm. Bligh*. Breadfruit plants would be dug up in Tahiti—he'd tasted the strange fruit when a native had traded one for a string of glass beads—and then be transported to the West Indies. There, the trees would feed the slaves, who had been brought from Africa to cut the sugarcane, which itself had been brought long ago from Asia to produce the sugar that was shipped to England and stirred into tea, itself shipped from China, unless Banks could get someone to steal the tea plants and grow them elsewhere—maybe Calcutta?—and surely he could induce Chinamen to migrate with their plants so that the whole operation would be in British control . . .

He drew elaborate arrows and lines, the globe spinning and spinning. And though these first grand efforts were doomed to fail—*Bounty* by mutiny, *Guardian* by iceberg—

Banks would not surrender. Soon he would, in the name of Empire, rearrange the living world.

Atlantic, 1799

JUST OUTSIDE the port of La Coruña, in a corvette called the *Pizarro,* a young German naturalist named Alexander von Humboldt was setting sail for Spanish America. A sensuous young man with romantic eyes and Napoleonic hair, he had read the accounts of Bougainville and Cook and had once met Banks for tea and admired his Pacific herbarium, and now he was launching his own journey of scientific discovery. He wished to plumb the secret unities of nature—to learn how living things gained a foothold on land, how land itself was created. Spanish America, with its volcanoes and jungles, had been well plundered but never really *known.* He traveled with barometers, sextants, chronometers, quadrants, a dipping needle, and a pendulum to measure the world he found; what he longed most to do, though, was embrace it, be moved to the fundaments of his soul. The device he brought that he cherished the most measured the blueness of the sky.

As the ship slowly crossed the Atlantic and sailed south, Humboldt charted the water currents and watched the constellations change. *A strange, completely unknown feeling is awoken in us when nearing the equator and crossing from one hemisphere to another,* he wrote in his journal. *The stars we have known since infancy begin to vanish.* At last he reached Venezuela.

There he saw fat night birds that lived in a cave, and river eels that electrified horses, and a beach called the Playa de

Huevos because so many turtles planted eggs in its sand that the natives could simply harvest them. He found seashells far from any sea and a pair of enormous thighbones the locals believed had belonged to a giant. He measured troubling subterranean fires, flames that lapped from the ground. And he saw springs of yellow petroleum bubbling up along the shore. Released, though, from where, from *what*? The smell was so strong, the bubbling so lively, a pity the stuff had no use.

As he struggled through the Amazon on mules and boats, he reflected that Man was not master in the Tropics but instead a transient guest wise to enjoy the fruits that were offered. He passed from the Torrid Zone to the Temperate, onward up to the Frigid, until he reached the high Andes. Cotopaxi, with its white cone brilliant against the blue sky, he found the most beautiful of all. At last he came to the city of Quito, high up on the equator. There he was a prized guest among Spanish colonial society. But at all the dinners and balls, Humboldt said just enough to entertain the ladies before fleeing to his roof to study the stars.

Finally he did what he had come for: he climbed Pichincha, the volcanic mountain that loomed over the city. Only a few years earlier it had erupted so violently that thousands of people had been buried alive or sucked into sudden crevices. He wished to look into Pichincha's crater, just as on an earlier journey he had descended into Vesuvius. It was really the only way to *see*: a hot little glimpse of how earth was made.

This climb took a day. High up at the barren, lunar peak, while the Indians and mules waited behind in the mist, Humboldt in his black boots and yellow velvet jacket stepped to the rim of Pichincha's crater. He marveled at his fortune, for as he stood there at the steaming maw, beneath his feet the mountain groaned. It shook. In thirty-six minutes it shook fifteen times, as if the ground floated on soup.

Neptunists believed all rock was sedimentary, created through the agency of water. Volcanists thought deep fires were involved.

Humboldt already knew that volcanoes spewed fish. Also that earthquakes occurred in chains—like beads in a necklace, he thought. He would call the Andes the *Avenue of Volcanoes*.

So matters of creation were becoming clearer; extraordinary connections were afoot.

PART I

I

THE BRANIFF that carried the Forders to Ecuador left Miami International at dusk. As the plane taxied down the runway, Alice held tight the glass flowers and beads she'd been allowed to buy at the airport now that her nickels would be useless, and when the plane lifted, she pressed her forehead to the window to see the Keys and the Caribbean and, with luck, a whale. But before they even reached the sea, the sun sank. Then there was nothing to see but the red light flashing on the wing, her own ghostly face in the oval of glass, and the blackness of space, the stars.

But the stars in Ecuador, Rosalind had said, would not be the same as the ones in Washington. More like the stars in Australia, more like home.

So could you notice when they changed?

EVEN BEFORE the Forders left Washington, they had known a situation awaited them in Ecuador. Hal had paced the living room and cracked his knuckles upon receiving the post and the news.

"There's been a power seizure," he said. "An *autogolpe*. I'll be damned." He sipped his scotch, looking over the rim of the glass at Rosalind, as Alice lay drawing on the floor.

Hal was tall and thin, with eyes the color of metal, and his hands were long. His teeth were long, too, like a dog's, and he had a tight, negotiating mouth.

He paused at the mantel and jiggled his ice. "Velasco Ibarra's seized dictatorial rule. Dismissed congress and the courts."

"What will it mean for us?" asked Rosalind. She sat straight in the big gold chair, looking up at him with worried gray eyes.

Hal shrugged. "*Estado de sitio,* most likely. Military rule for a while." He was silent a moment, then smiled. "It's interesting. Very interesting. An interesting time to be there."

AT DAWN THE PLANE was flying above what seemed to be towering clouds, immaterial. But when slanting sun rays struck the clouds, they suddenly became ice and giant, sharp rock.

"The Avenue of Volcanoes," announced the pilot. "In a minute we'll fly over Cotopaxi."

Everyone was waking up, sliding open the small plastic blinds. Alice pressed her nose to the glass and stared down at the shocking landscape of peaks. She was nine, and this would be her fourth country, sixth city, seventh house. And she had only just become conscious, as a human being is said to be conscious, aware of itself in a place and time. The sensation kept burning through her like light. Everything seemed astonishing, precarious.

"There she blows!" said the pilot, as the plane flew alongside a huge conical mountain. "Have a look at Cotopaxi. Highest active volcano in the world."

It seemed unbelievably near. Its peak was all snow, the sides creased and veined, and they were flying so close you could almost reach out and touch the gleaming white surface. Then the plane climbed up above the peak and wheeled, and Alice stared down into the steaming crater.

A huge white hole, inhuman, compelling. You could just run around its rim, down its deep creases, and in.

Quito lay high on a plateau in the Andes, in the lap of Mount Pichincha. It seemed small and unreal as the plane approached, a city nestled in the folded, jagged landscape. As they flew closer, tiny buildings with red or white roofs appeared, spreading out in the high valley and rising a little way up Pichincha's slopes, before they gave way to patchwork fields, green and brown and yellow. Then the fields stopped, leaving only the mountain's bare brown flanks, which rose to a stony peak. Some of the fields were burning, smoke drifting into the deep blue sky.

Scattered throughout the city as the plane flew over, inside large houses safe behind gates, American children whose parents worked for the State Department or Texaco were lying in their bedrooms. They read *American Girl* or listened to *Abbey Road* or other new records their fathers had brought back from R & R, or they wrote passionate letters on paper decorated with frogs to the friends they'd left behind at the last post, friends they'd never see again and would soon replace.

On the edge of town, at the airport, where the streets were unfinished and turned back into dirt, a crowd of

Ecuadorians waited, as they waited every day, for the flight to come in.

THE PLANE BEGAN to descend, and everything quickly became larger. Rosalind, Hal, and all the other embassy and oil people pushed their blankets to the floor, freshened their faces, and adjusted their watches; stewardesses bustled; babies screamed. Then everyone looked out the oval windows as the plane sank and the city grew real. They were about to arrive in a foreign country again—Spanish already, the new place already—and wasn't it awfully *bright* out there.

In the airport, Hal and the other American fathers led the way through immigration and baggage claim. When they reached the glass doors, the crowd of Ecuadorians on the other side pushed forward, a crowd the Americans could hardly make out, just a mass of color and darkness. When the glass doors opened, though, they smelled it.

Urine and smoke, wailing and chanting, begging hands missing fingers and crusted with dirt, brown faces, black hats, black hair, pink and green and yellow clothing. People who seemed to be on their knees were not on their knees, they did not have knees, they sat with stumps in wagons, reaching and moaning.

"Por favor, Señor, Señorita, por favor . . ."

Rosalind pressed Alice's shoulders. "Just go," she whispered. "Hang on to Hal."

Hal's head moved high above the bright colors and dark faces, and Alice gripped his thumb and followed until they reached a car with a man waiting beside it, a tall freckled man, his collar open.

Hal pulled his hand free of Alice's and shook. "Tom, good to see you. Rosalind, Alice, say hello to Tom Mueller. Tom, my wife and her daughter."

"Welcome," said Mr. Mueller. "Good flight?"

Rosalind smiled weakly and threw up her hands.

"It's always awful," he said. "We'll take you straight to the house."

Everything was shockingly bright. The place could not be closer to the sun, the air could not be more rare. The car whizzed along wide avenues and steep narrow streets, past plazas and fountains, baroque churches alongside sleek white buildings alongside green pastures and huts, palm trees like pineapples, fat buses and telephone posts, cows being herded, and dogs. Hal leaned forward and spoke with Tom Mueller and then made a joke to the driver in Spanish, as if the language came with the air. Everything seemed to be rocking. Alice clutched the door handle and tried not to vomit.

"All right," Hal said as they pulled up to a gate. "Here we are. *La casa.*"

THE HOUSE WAS LARGE, pale yellow stucco, with purple flowers climbing the walls and a roof of terra-cotta tiles; all the windows, even upstairs, had black iron bars, and around the house stood a high stone wall, upon which broken glass glittered. In the garden were palm trees, lush grass, beds of flowers, and the steps that led from the garden to the house were flat slabs of granite. A dark man in white waited there; behind him, through the open door, lay deep shadowy space and then bright squares that were the back windows opening to the mountains and blazing sky. Rosalind smiled and squeezed Alice's hand as they got out of the car: on a post again, proceeding!

The house had been lived in by the family they were replacing, Mr. Mueller told them, so he knew his way around. "The reception area, the living room," he said, as he strode through large spaces smelling of paint.

There were fireplaces large enough to crawl into, crawl up. Their furniture had already arrived, the tasseled brown-and-gold rug, the black leather table, the big gold chair. The things traveled with them everywhere, as brave and sturdy as Rosalind said they themselves were, living this life. Like turtles, she said, carrying our little homes with us. Each year for Alice seemed to dwell in its own house and sometimes even its own country, so that you moved through space as well as time, and then it all evaporated behind you like smoke. Except for the things, which were more constant.

The carved whale tooth already lay on the black leather table, where it usually was. As Mr. Mueller showed Hal a detail of the window lock, Alice went over and sat on the sofa and took the whale tooth and held it, as she always did when they first arrived. It was bigger than her hand, polished and heavy as stone, gently curving, like an elephant tusk or a bull horn. For a moment she tried to remember if a whale tooth was bone or ivory, or just the same as her own teeth. She shut her eyes, the tooth heavy and cold in her hand, and instead pictured it still planted in the mouth of its whale, the huge blue creature somewhere deep, swimming.

"Formal dining room," Mr. Mueller was saying. He pointed to a swinging door. "You've got two kitchens, which you'll need, and double pantries, too. Now let me just see if the staff is ready—" He disappeared through the swinging door.

"Remember," Rosalind whispered to Alice, "in countries like this, one has servants. As we did in São Miguel, with your father. Although you were too young to remember, weren't you. And in countries like this, one has bars on the windows, because one has to be a little more careful."

Mr. Mueller returned, followed by three people. The stocky young man who had stood at the door was Manuel, who would be the houseboy.

"A terrible word, isn't it," said Rosalind. He bowed.

Next was a round older woman the color of baked bread, with a white apron over a blue dress, and warm brown eyes that drooped, and earrings dangling from long, stretched lobes.

"This must be Maria," said Rosalind. "*¿Sí?* She will be our cook."

And a young woman with high cheekbones and nervous eyes was Rosita—

"Carlita," said Hal.

"Oh yes," said Rosalind. "Forgive me. Such a long flight and everything new. Carlita, Carlita."

She would dust things, carry glasses, offer canapés on silver trays. And outside, bent in the garden in the sun, was José. Palm fronds and banana leaves rustled over his head.

"You are to be very polite to these people," said Rosalind, as Maria, Manuel, and Carlita went back through the swinging door. "You are to continue making your own bed."

"Quichuan," said Hal, with satisfaction. "You can see those Indian features at once."

"Look at the woodwork of these banisters," said Tom Mueller, as he led the way upstairs. "And just wait until you see the bread-dough dolls, the weaving."

ALICE'S ROOM was at the end of a broad hall and faced the street. It had a balcony, and she'd never had a balcony before; she also had hopes for the closet. The doorknob was foreign, they always were, along with the faucets and light switches. But you got used to them, like the language. *¿Cómo está usted?* She had a notebook already full of sentences. *¡Buenos días! Me llamo Alice Forder.*

The name itself she still practiced, as it was only a year old; before, she had been Alice Carroll. And her nationality she now checked on school forms as *U.S.*, although she printed *(born in Australia)*.

She went into the closet to see how it was. This one was deep and had built-in drawers. She pulled them out and adjusted them so that they formed a sort of staircase, and climbed up. At the top, above where the clothes would hang, was a broad shelf like a bunk bed. There was just enough space to sit up and swing her legs. When she lay back, it seemed pleasantly to rock and lull, as if she were still on the plane, or a train, or a ship.

DOWNSTAIRS, down the long hallway and the curving staircase, Hal Forder was saying good-bye to Tom Mueller. Around the corner, Rosalind Forder (née Edwards, then Carroll) stood considering the reception-room space. And around the globe, far away, Rupert Carroll was perhaps at that moment writing Alice a letter on a sheet of paper with a tiny engraved emu and kangaroo at the top.

Of her father Alice mostly had letters. The engraving on the letterhead she once cut out and put in her wallet, for it seemed to contain both father and country, and when she looked at that miniature kangaroo and emu she felt something: a crucial kinship. Sometimes, the name of the place seemed enough—*Australia*—as if the word itself was *her*. And its shape on the map, an orange island in the wide blue sea: that, too, somehow was her.

Of Australia itself she had mementos. A book, with a picture of a monster called the Banksia Man. He was covered with what looked like barnacles and stood at the edge of a cliff, about to hurl a gumnut baby into the ocean. But the baby proved to be adaptable; it could breathe underwater and swam clear to another world. Alice also remembered a few things: the smell of gum trees on a picnic; boulders that jutted from the sand like the spine and tail of a buried dinosaur. And she had a stuffed kangaroo, from her grandmother Violet. Vi had given it to her out on the tarmac at Adelaide airport, when Alice and Rosalind were leaving Australia for good, although Alice didn't know this. The wind blew Vi's thin gray hair and turned the freckles on her skinny arms to goose bumps. Her lopsided eyes, just like Alice's, watered as she pressed the kangaroo into Alice's arms. "Now *remember*," she'd whispered, clutching Alice close and breathing quick at her ear. "Don't ever forget! You must always remember where you're *from*."

A SQUARE OF LIGHT suddenly opened in the closet beside Alice.

"The place seems all right," said Hal. "Decent closets."

There was a jingling of hangers, a rustle. Through a small vent hole Alice could see straight into the master bedroom, out to the porch, and beyond.

"So you heard Mueller," Hal said. "Velasco only pulled off this power grab because of his nephew, Acosta. You can't do this sort of thing without the military behind you. But I don't know, Acosta seems weak. And if he can't deliver the military—"

Hal laughed, the hangers jingling. "Then your bet's as good as mine how long Velasco holds the country."

Then he must have shut the door, leaving that lingering bright square in the darkness.

$\mathcal{T}$HE WATER was not to be drunk.

"When brushing teeth, never swallow," said Rosalind, as all the mothers on the first day said, reading from an embassy pamphlet that Maria had just brought upstairs. They stood on Rosalind and Hal's balcony, the terra-cotta tiles hot beneath Alice's feet. Beyond Rosalind, beyond her wavy hair all lit like a halo while that same intense light made her face dark, were the tops of the palm trees in the garden. And beyond them were the mountain, the deep sky.

"Probably a few drops of water won't kill you," said Rosalind. "But all the same, mind out."

And you weren't to go barefoot, either. Rosalind looked down at Alice's feet. "Although it's not altogether clear why," she said. "Some sort of parasitic something, I suppose. So shoes on! Except for inside the house, and surely the balconies are all right, and perhaps within our own garden walls," she said. "That's all right, wouldn't you think?"

She looked at Alice, and then at Maria, who raised her eyebrows and hands, helpless. "Well," said Rosalind, "let's just say not. The ground is the ground, after all."

The ground, the water, the walls spiked with glass. Like the other fathers, Hal went early in the morning to the embassy. The ambassador and deputy ambassador and attachés varied the route they drove each morning. One had to be careful. Unlike the others, though, the Forders did not live up in the hills but in town, and the embassy was only five blocks away. So Hal walked to work, bold, eyes appraising. He liked to feel he was really in the place, he said, so he would know its measure. His Spanish was excellent, and he saw exactly what was before him, having no time for anything lower or higher. He was a man other men admired. Even Alice could see this, and when he had first appeared two years earlier, she moved tentatively near, until at last he noticed her, and patted her head. When he bought a new car, it would be powerful. He'd have an El Dorado, he said, which would make sense, wouldn't it, given where they now lived. A pale blue convertible that he would drive with one hand all over the lush country, cigarette smoke blowing into the landscape and mixing with the trail of exhaust.

When the gate clanged securely behind him, Rosalind turned in the front hall to face the staff. What should be prepared for lunch and dinner, which entailed what should be bought, and how she wished the house to be kept, and the table set, and the phone answered, and the clothes laundered, and there was always the question of flowers. Her Spanish dictionary grew soft and worn as she hunted through it and brightly produced one word after another, while Maria, Carlita, and Manuel stood patiently before her in their uniforms. But this time truly she would do it, she said, it would not be like it had been with Rupert, when everything had just been too much.

Rosalind had beautiful strong legs Hal liked to see danc-ing, and sea-gray eyes, often weeping, or reckless. She had pounded the steering wheel at night in Australia before plunging into the new marriage and the new nationality. She just wanted, she said, to get *away*.

SCHOOL WOULDN'T START for another week, so Alice wan-dered in the garden. It was a little above the street, a bed of bright green grass between the yellow house and the stone wall studded with broken glass. Along the wall stood snap-dragons, and other flowers Alice didn't know, and it was strange the way some things seemed familiar—a certain shrub with watery blue blossoms; a palm tree with a skinny, scaly trunk and a wild head of fronds at the top. But familiar from where? She rocked on her sneakers in the warm, sinking grass, and squinted up at the palm against that shocking blue sky, and it seemed always that the past lay just behind or be-neath her, drifting off in layers, and once you moved on it was gone, and could never be gripped and retrieved. Maybe that palm tree had been in Australia?

But the mountain, rising up high beyond the house and its terra-cotta roof, high beyond the palm tree: Pichincha. It was completely new. It stood huge and jagged and motion-less, yet the way the clouds floated behind its stony peak, it looked as though it kept approaching, slowly moving toward her. She had to keep looking back to check.

THE CURFEW WAS still on, so at dinner, as they sat in the din-ing room in the high-backed chairs, the city glinted silently through the barred windows. No cars on the street, no buses, no people. Carlita came through the swinging door with her eyes fixed upon a tureen in both hands. When she ladled the soup, it looked as though she did it without breathing, moving cautiously in her small white sneakers as Hal's eyes followed her hands. First *la señora,* then *la niña,* then *el señor.* And she was done, without a spill. She broke into a smile, flushed, and hurried back through the door.

"Excellent," said Hal, after blowing and tasting. "She makes a terrific potato soup, that Maria."

Rosalind looked pleased.

"Must be some sort of traditional recipe," he said. "Potatoes are very important up here, you know. You should learn some things before school starts, Alice. The things that are important to the country. Bananas, fish, timber, coffee, cocoa, sugar. And of course," he added, "oil."

"What, vegetable?" said Rosalind.

"Of course not vegetable, what do you think. Petroleum. Been pumping a little out from the shore near Guayaquil for decades, but in the last few years"—he pointed with an elbow—"over there in the Oriente, too. A *lot* of oil. Boom time. It'll rocket the place into development. Texaco and Gulf negotiated some very nice concessions a few years back, and I can tell you there are people here who are not happy about that. Oil will outweigh all the other exports within a year, the place'll develop fast. A wonder if Velasco will be able to manage it."

Everyone spooned soup. The city was silent.

"A wonder if this curfew will ever end," said Rosalind.

"So tell me. Alice. What's the highest mountain?"

She had in fact read this. "Chimborazo?"

Hal was pleased. "Good girl. Twenty thousand six hundred."

"Meters?" said Rosalind.

"Of course not. Feet. Nearly twenty-one thousand feet."

"Goodness," said Rosalind. "And what are we?"

"Well Alice might make four one day, and even with those heels I'd say you're still under six."

"Oh, oh."

"Up here in Quito we're nine thousand. Thereabouts. That's why the air's so thin. Pichincha's fifteen or so. I tell you, though, it's altogether different down at the coast. Hot and wet. We'll go down sometime. Maybe Christmas."

"Christmas!" said Rosalind. "Is that the season?" She beamed at Alice. "Just like at home, then, just like Australia."

Hal wiped his mouth. "Try," he said, "Rosalind, to remember that you're part of the American service now."

EVEN THOUGH Rosalind had given up her own and Alice's citizenship when she married Hal, they still had their accents, and Alice's glittered hopefully around her at Académia Cotopaxi the first day.

She would wait for the school bus across the street, Rosalind had showed her where. Out the heavy front door, past the bougainvillea, hydrangeas, pineapple palm, and fig tree, through the gate, once Manuel had pushed the button inside to open it, and then into another world. There the street smelled of urine, dogs sniffed in the gutters, and up by the *bodega* men knocked a soccer ball with their foreheads and knees and looked over when they heard the gate clang shut behind her. A truck with crates of Orange Crush bottles jangled by; cars honked out tunes at the walled corners before rushing through. A boy with black hair and one leg shorter than the other limped from the house on the opposite corner and waited for a bus to his own school, glancing once at Alice. An ancient woman in a broad-rimmed black hat and bright pink poncho crept along the sidewalk by the stone walls, stopping at each gate, pushing the intercom button, and then chanting, swaying, her hands begging even though there was no one to see, until the electric crackling was cut off, and she fell silent and moved on.

When the bus came, it was empty, Alice was the first to be picked up, and this was lucky as she could sit safe in the back. The Number Seven zoomed down the avenues, weaving among the local buses, which were fat and had men clinging to the sides and crates of chickens strapped on top, while her own bus was sleek and sealed. It skimmed past white buildings, palm trees, churches, beggars, dead dogs lying in gutters; it whizzed past the embassy with its tall white walls, marines with guns resting on their shoulders, and the flag waving against the sky that was such a deep liquid blue. On Pichincha the fields were smoking; in the distance were the peaks of Cayambe and Cotopaxi, far and white and spectacular, and it was hard not to think about that crater up there, and how you could just run in.

One by one children got on, but the first few seemed to be new, like her; each looked around apprehensively, then slid into a private seat. But soon others were picked up and the bus filled with noise.

"So do you like it here, in Ecki-dor?" one of the knowing children asked.

Alice shrugged. "It's all right." She held her hands together.

"You mean Icki-dor," a boy shouted. He had a crew cut and quick eyes, and he swung down the aisle between seats. Now he came swinging before Alice, and put his red sneakers up on her armrests. "That's what we call it. Because of the Ickies."

The buses reached the Académia's gates and went through. Then the children poured out onto the soccer field, and all the usual began again. Within the white walls, on the other side of which Ecuadorian children their own age without shoes were herding cows with sticks, the American boys and girls stood in little circles and began to establish the ranks—the obvious rank based on the fathers, and the real rank based on themselves. Smartest girl in the class! Funniest boy! There had finally been proof at the last post, but it would have to be established all over again.

"So what's your father?" a girl asked Alice. The girls here seemed much older than the ones in Washington. They wore bell-bottoms and earrings and shirts with flaring sleeves, and one named Celeste had ice-blue eye shadow.

Hal was a deputy something, Alice knew. "But," she added, "he's not really my father."

The girls nodded knowingly but still with some interest. "So where's your real one?"

"Australia."

They considered her. "Then you're Australian, too."

She nodded, wondering if that were true.

"You don't really look American, you know."

"No," a plump girl named Candi said, gazing at Alice with her head tilted. "She doesn't. I think she looks more Australian."

"So what's Australia like?" said Celeste. "Haven't been there yet."

Alice realized that she didn't know. Kangaroos and emus: they were common, in zoos. What could she say, then? Rupert's freckled hands? The smell of the gum trees? The Banksia Man in the book?

But Celeste and the other fourth graders had already turned away; they had seen so many places, after all.

Overhead the Braniff soared, insect-green that day.

SITTING AT HER DESK in homeroom, Alice concentrated, trying to learn who was who. Michelle had curly black hair and her eyes were soft as a cow's; Celeste with the eye shadow looked like Snow White; Dexter was crew cut, a little marine, the one who shouted and swung on the bus; Mark had long white-blond hair and a crooked grin; Candi was plump and her front teeth were crossed, but she twisted around in her chair and smiled at Alice.

On the first day already charm bracelets flashed and jingled as hectic notes were scribbled, folded, and surreptitiously delivered. Some were tossed, jaunty, by those with good aim; others were passed from one hot hand to the next. Alice had to pass three, Celeste on one side and a red-haired boy on the other making desperate faces to show her which way secretly to hand them. So the messages flew around the classroom, establishing alliances, hatreds, trysts. As if these nine-year-olds were butterflies and must accomplish everything fast because there was so little time—or as if, with all the traveling they'd done, they'd lost their proper sense of time, like fruit from another hemisphere trying to ripen too soon.

"WE MUST REMIND YOU," said the health teacher, "especially those of you who are new, never to drink the water. If you look at a drop under the microscope, you'll see that it's full of living things."

"What are they, anyway?" Alice whispered to the boy beside her.

"Worms," he said. He lowered his lids and smiled. "Don't you know? Tiny, microscopic worms that go in your mouth and settle inside you and eat all your food after you've eaten it and grow until they've filled your intestines. But they have to come out for air sometimes, from your nose. Or even," he whispered, close to her ear, "from your butt hole."

"Come on," said Alice.

He smiled. "So drink it."

"You must not drink the water in any form," Miss Higgins was saying. "Now, what is another form water can take?"

"Ice!" someone cried.

"Indeed. And you never know," she went on, twirling her pointer, "where they get the water to make the popsicles they sell on the street."

But down the hall the geography teacher, Mr. Peterson, said, "What a stupendous place this is!" His blue eyes sparkled behind his glasses, and he had a curly beard. The same ginger hair was on his toes, in sandals. Pictures and maps were pinned all over his room: a green thundering waterfall, a hot black island.

"Have you ever seen such mountains?" he said. "Have you ever seen such a sky?"

BUT THE SKY lost its light quickly, there on the equator. Then the city lay glittering in the mountain's lap, its lights mirrored by the stars. It didn't seem possible, as Alice stood on the balcony and stared up, that there could be so many stars. As if, were you to pull away the veil of black, all that light would fall.

It was quiet, then, still no one allowed on the streets. But as Alice was gazing up at the sky in the hills all around, where the modern houses stood, the first of the season's initiations took place.

Earlier, before curfew, mothers had waited in their cars for the gate to open, for their girls to slip from the cars and run in. Then the girls had played Twister and told ghost stories, and grown hot with sugar and excitement, until the hosting mother came in and told them lights-out. In the fuggy air of sleeping bags and breath, after several eruptions of giggling, it gradually became quiet.

But after a time, a set of girls who had only pretended to sleep opened their eyes and looked at each other over the slumbering bodies, as planned. They silently crawled from their sleeping bags toward the girl they had earlier chosen. They drew close, kneeling around her in their nightgowns, and, with eyes intent, one on each side began to unbutton her pajamas: the top button, the second, the third. They slid her little flannel top open. Then, with excruciating slowness, they slipped their hands under the elasticized waist and inched her pajama bottoms down. No farther than the thighs, though, it didn't matter any farther. They drew back and looked.

What concerned them was the state of development. It was just curiosity, nothing more. It was something they needed to know. They studied the smooth chest, the pale nipples, the hairless cleft between slender hips. Each girl looked on at the little landscape, making her own crucial comparisons.

When they had seen enough, they looked at one another. Then they gave the girl a tickling squeeze, to signal that she'd passed her ravishment.

"THE THING TO DO," Candi later told Alice, as the two sat by the tetherball ring with their lunch bags, "is just let them do it. Pretend you're asleep."

Candi looked like an owl. She had a heart mouth and round tortoiseshell glasses, and Alice believed her, but still she said, "Why?"

"Because if you don't let them do it, you'll be out. But if you do—you're automatically *in*."

3

"THE THING TO DO," Mr. Peterson told the fourth graders, "is see all that you can while you're here. You're in an astonishing part of the world!"

He beamed and raised himself up on his toes, as if he wanted to fly out of the room that minute and explore. He wore hiking boots and jeans and a woven Ecuadorian belt; a poncho hung over his chair, its little green pom-poms dangling.

"The Amazon, for instance," he said. "Where you'll find parrots and snakes and pumas, electric eels and monkeys. The Galápagos! Blue-footed boobies, giant tortoises, iguanas."

"Iguanas," said Celeste, wrinkling her nose.

"They're like small dinosaurs, don't you want to see a dinosaur? And besides all that, there's the Andes."

"Volcanoes!" shouted Dexter.

"Certainly, volcanoes. But can you imagine how things look from up there? All that ice right on the equator, underneath this blazing sky. Can you imagine climbing that high, standing on top of the world?"

Mr. Peterson himself climbed them. Alice could see, when he spoke, those mountains like clouds in his pale blue eyes, as if once you'd been up there you were burned, imprinted.

"THE THING TO DO," Hal told Rosalind and Alice, "is get to know the right kind of people."

They were driving out to the hacienda of a contact he'd made, a local, upper-echelon, very good man to know. The hacienda was halfway around Pichincha, and the new convertible flew over rutted, stony roads as Hal steered with one hand, smoke streaming from his nostrils. They drove through fields of sugarcane and pineapple, and through banana plantations, the long ragged leaves and heavy bruised fruit hanging down dense around them. As one set of mountains receded, new mountains appeared; it was like being in a sea, a huge green wave always swelling up beyond the one that had just crashed behind them. All around, the land soared and dipped and buckled, sometimes looking as if huge slabs of it had tilted up, nothing flat anywhere, wild. Once it hailed, tiny balls of ice like pumice bouncing upon their heads, but by the time Hal pulled over to put up the top, they'd gone through. Alice got out and saw that there was a line across the road: on one side it was wet and hailing, while the other side was sunny. They passed crumbling mud huts surrounded by spiky plants and fires; dogs ran out, chickens flapped, people in black hats looked up. Once a horse was grazing so near a fire it was surely feeding on flames.

They stopped to buy pineapples. A brown man in short white pants cut a fruit free with a machete, hacked away the prickly sides, and held out the pale core to Alice. Her chin dripped sweet juice as they drove on.

"Tell me again, I'm sorry, what's his name?" asked Rosalind after they drove through a cobblestoned village and pulled up to a tall iron gate.

"Cabeza de Vaca. Jorge."

"Cabeza de Vaca, how could I forget. And it means what I think?"

At the end of a gravel drive lined with trees was an old white colonial house. Saddles hung in a hallway smelling of leather and horse; sheepskins lay on the shining wood floor, over which Rosalind's high-heeled sandals clattered. She laughed as Señor Cabeza de Vaca kissed her hand.

"Come in, come in, *bienvenidos.*"

"Terrific place," said Hal, and whistled through his teeth.

There were pastures for bulls and cows, which stretched partway up the mountain; there were groves of gum trees, bees for honey, and even a ring for bullfights.

"Some of the Americans like that," said Señor Cabeza de Vaca. "Yes, they enjoy it, we use just the heifers. A few men in oil, one or two from the embassy. Perhaps you'd like to try, sometime?"

Hal pulled a droll face and said he'd sure as hell watch, while Rosalind laughed and declared that she'd dare it.

They had lunch, tostadas and grilled chicken and something soft wrapped in hot corn husks. Cream sat on Alice's milk.

"Tell me, Alicia, can you ride?"

"She can sure learn," said Hal. "Can't you, Alice? With all those gymnastics and climbing you do."

"Well then, I have a very nice horse for you."

A girl named Claudia who worked in the stables led the horse out and helped Alice on. When she had mounted her own, she smiled showily and gestured with her reins and the heels of her boots to demonstrate how things were done. Then she laughed, slapped Alice's horse, and the two took off.

"Famoso," she called from behind. *"El caballo se llama Famoso."*

Famoso? Formosa? Alice clung to the horse with her legs, with her hands, gripping the horn of the saddle, the coarse mane. The horse cantered along the road out of the hacienda, into the village. Claudia was behind her, then beside her, and then she laughed and dug in her heels, and both horses suddenly galloped. They veered away from the road and into the lush open fields, the hooves now drumming soft earth. Claudia's horse sprang, and Alice's own horse tightened and leapt before she had even seen the stream, and for a hanging, silent moment, they flew. Then again they were pounding through grass, just the steady thudding of hooves, and she clung to the horse's side and mane as it galloped, and the air rushed around her so fast she barely breathed, she seemed to be air itself. They raced over the field, into a wood, back out into the sloping green.

At last they stopped. Alice slid from the sweating horse into the grass, knee-deep and slippery as silk.

"Bien," said Claudia, pushing back her hair with a dirty hand.

Beside them the horses tore mouthfuls of grass. Alice lay breathless, ecstatic, staring up at the sky.

They returned more slowly. The horses ambled, side by side. As they passed through the alley of trees that lined the drive to the hacienda, Claudia reached up and pulled an avocado from a branch. Alice strained in the stirrups to reach for one, too. The other girl snapped off the stem, poked it through the leathery skin, squeezed, and out came smooth pale paste.

"¿*Paraíso, no?*" said Claudia, wiping the green from her mouth.

"HELL OF A MESS," said Hal as they sped home to be in time for curfew. The air was cool, the sky just beginning to lose light, the fields around them smoking.

"Hell of a mess Velasco's got himself into with these import taxes, not to mention the expropriations. Can't imagine what he thinks he's doing. How can someone be president four times and still be such a fool. Plus he's not budging on the China vote. And the word is, if he won't work with us, the hell with him. It's not only us he's aggravating but some pretty important people down here. He'll have to make it up somehow."

Rosalind's eyes were shut, one arm hanging out over the door, her hand open to the breeze. "Just smell those gum trees," she said. "And the jacaranda. Now it'll really seem like Christmas, when the jacaranda's in bloom, all blue."

"But the interesting thing," Hal went on, "the really interesting thing will be to see exactly how Velasco does it."

4

For the time being, though, all Velasco did was cancel the curfew, so the Americans were free. Suddenly the phone in the big yellow house was always ringing, and engraved invitations appeared on the entranceway table. Hal and Rosalind and the other Americans spilled from their gates for dinners and dances.

The children were allowed to have parties, too, just like the ones their parents gave. Alice practiced dancing with Candi up on Candi's cindery roof.

"So you like it here, in Ecki-dor?" Candi was from Texas. Her father worked for Texaco, and she had been here two years already. They were trying to dance as they had seen women do when they watched through banisters, through bars.

Each night before you go to bed, my baby, whisper a little prayer for me, my baby . . .

They clasped each other, lowered their lids and childish lashes, swung their narrow hips, snapped their fingers.

"Now you be Dexter," said Candi.

"No, you be Mark."

"Okay, but like *this*."

"Okay."

They pressed their soft cheeks together and shut their eyes, Alice's nose in Candi's brown hair and Candi's in Alice's dirty-blond, one girl's leg between the other's, shifting around and around with little steps.

In the darkness black moths as big as their hands fluttered, and every now and then one brushed their cheeks, leaving soft sooty scales. Far above, nearer than they'd ever been, the stars glittered, and Alice stared up as Candi pressed her head near her own and they kept moving around and around.

"You really like it here, in Ecki-dor, don't you?" whispered Candi, pulling away then and gazing up, too.

But the word *like* was so small. The girls sat down, side by side on a chimney, and stared at the night sky until they were dizzy. You could not even see the stars' patterns anymore, they were lost in the sheer volume, the brilliance.

THE SAME MUSIC played at the children's parties as at their parents' because there was nothing but the few records brought back from R & R: the Mamas and the Papas, Herb Alpert, Three Dog Night, The Guess Who. *No sugar tonight in my coffee, no sugar tonight in my tea!* The parents sipped martinis upstairs while the children drank Orange Crush in the basement, but they all danced, slow danced. Little girls wearing white boots and hot pants draped their thin arms around the necks of boys who held themselves militarily erect. They gyrated their hips and swung beads with peace-sign and heart medallions, and they played spin the bottle and kissed on sofas in large new or Spanish colonial houses, behind high walls spiked with glass.

———

On WEEKENDS the families drove all over the country. Alice gazed up from the back of the convertible at the white peaks stretching off in all directions. The country was an ocean of land, unfolding. Squinting into the blazing sun, she left her mother and the Bachrachs and the O'Donnells on a picnic by a river one Sunday, a river that a few weeks earlier had been violent but now was dry. It was just a broad gully of stones scattered on baked clay. She found a skull of something lodged in the rocks, but it was all white and clean. She picked it up with both hands and held it to the light and looked at the blue sky shining through the eyeholes, but she couldn't tell what animal it had come from. She propped it on top of a rock and climbed deeper into the dry river, stepping from rock to rock until she crossed to the other side. She climbed up the bank, pulling herself by gripping roots and long handfuls of grass. And she kept going, on and on, wading knee-deep through a silky meadow, and never reached an end, never found anything to make her turn back. A gorge, a lagoon whose water was black with tadpoles: there was no reason to stop and she could not get enough. Finally she dropped into the deep grass and gathered long moist armfuls about her and lay there. Only the voice of her mother, far behind, made her rise from that sweet soft earth.

And WHEN, ONE NIGHT at a slumber party, it was finally Alice's turn, she lay still atop her silken sleeping bag, as Candi had told her to do. She had almost been asleep, but when the girls stealthily gathered around, their sheer intensity woke her, their breath, as if she were a flame and flickered. Then like a flame she burned, neither breathing nor moving as her clothes were removed and she could feel them studying her body, her eyes shut for the thrill.

AFTER CHRISTMAS, Velasco decided what to do.

"I'll be damned," said Hal, cracking his knuckles as he came out to his and Rosalind's porch.

"What's happened?" said Rosalind. "Carlita, yes, please, you can put that down just over there. *Gracias.* Isn't it bright out here. Alice, here's your Crush. But what's happened?"

"That shrewd son of a bitch has figured out how to save face." Hal took a glass of beer from the tray on the little round table and stood a moment, smoking, the equatorial light blazing behind him. "They've seized one of our boats," he said.

"One of what boats? Come under the umbrella, I can hardly see you."

"Tuna boats. A fishing boat flying the United States flag. The Ecuadorians have got the balls to say we're fishing in their waters."

"Well! Are we?"

"Of course not, why would we do that. We're fishing in international waters. Highly migratory fish. They did this sort of thing before, a few years back. You'd think they'd have learned their lesson." He smiled.

"So," she said, "what happened?"

He shrugged and crossed his arms. "Coup."

Rosalind looked at him, said nothing.

After a moment he went on. "They seize our boat with a military gunship, then they slap on a nasty fine. Velasco's got *cojones,* I tell you. One hundred percent demagoguery."

"But why are they doing it? If it's not their water?"

"Just what I said earlier. To save face. He's got to stand tough to someone to hide how he's screwing up here, he's showing off for the OAS. I told you, he'd been holding out on the Taiwan vote to twist our arm for a new agreement, but he just didn't get his way, did he. Plus it'll bring in some income, those fines. But I tell you"—Hal paused, shook his head slowly, and exhaled—"the man's got very bad judgment."

"Well, I still don't understand how they can do it at all if it isn't their water. But what does it mean for now?"

"It means," said Hal, "that it will be very, very interesting if he keeps it up."

The Braniff appeared, red that day. Rosalind, Alice, and Hal all watched as it rose from the airport and angled over the city, its stream cutting Pichincha in two.

"Anyone going today?" asked Rosalind.

"Macintyre."

"Oh, already? They said they couldn't come to the party next month, but I didn't realize they were going so soon. But should we worry, I mean, about this boat?"

Hal laughed and stubbed out his cigarette. "Well, it is an act of hostility."

"But will anything change? Another, what was it called, *de sitio*?"

"No, everything's just the same. At least we'll certainly make it look that way."

"But meanwhile?"

He laughed again. "Meanwhile. An interesting time to be here."

5

*E*VERYTHING *was* exactly the same. Carnival, for instance, took place without incident. Of course it was a local thing, said the mothers, but the children always enjoyed it, and thank heavens there was no trouble, despite all that nonsense with tuna fish.

Water balloons flew everywhere. Green, yellow, purple, pink, they soared over the streets, spinning and wobbling. They appeared from high stone walls, from speeding cars, from buses, from hidden porches. People ran, hysterical, shielding their heads.

"For goodness' sake," said the Acadêmia teachers, "keep your mouths shut if one hits you in the face!"

For the balloons were filled not only with water, which was bad enough, but often with water mixed with flour, or even flour mixed with urine. They flew from everywhere, suddenly spinning toward you and slapping with a shock on your head, on your back, as you darted from a wall to a tree.

The Académia bus tore down the avenues, and balloons flew from all sides toward the windows. Alice and Michelle and Candi and even Dexter once, though he hid it with a hoot, screamed with as much abandon as they did on Saturdays in the embassy watching Dracula movies, as the pink or red balloons hurtled toward them and splatted against the glass.

And likewise, as if there were no altercations far out at sea, causing terse exchanges not only in Quito but in Washington and the United Nations as well, the parents had their parties, with plenty of locals invited, as that was the reason they were *there* after all. The Forders would have one soon, their first party since arriving. Rosalind's first party since marrying Hal; she'd been planning it for weeks.

And the children's parties continued, too, and the music, Joe Cocker and the Mamas and the Papas. *Each night before you go to bed, my baby . . .* Slow dancing, nine-year-old Mark brushed his hairless cheek and lips against nine-year-old Celeste's neck. Dexter and Candi kissed on a sofa, under a blanket, their lips eagerly nibbling. And Alice danced, too, a glass of Sprite in one hand as she swayed her narrow shoulders and hips, as she'd seen mothers do with martinis. She let Gavin put his hand casually on her back as she stood talking with other girls. And then, when they sat down on the sofa in a dark corner, she let him put his hand on her knee. She was wearing a zip-up skirt, and she sat, her slight body motionless and feeling nothing but the thrill, as his hand inched up the zipper. All over the dark basement sticky little hands with mother-clipped fingernails were sliding up girls' shirts and rubbing smooth chests, as if rubbing them into ripeness.

After the parties, Hal and the other fathers picked the children up. Then, all over this colonial city high in the Andes, a city that had been there for hundreds of years, the capital of a kingdom that was called *Ecuador* only when the Europeans renamed it in honor of what they'd learned about the globe, lights sparkled beneath the dark sparkling sky, and white-suited Quichuan houseboys pushed little buttons inside doors, and gates creaked open to admit American cars, as tiny green frogs hopped in the headlights.

"So do you like it here, in Ecki-dor?" was what the children still asked, what they would ask Alice until she was no longer new but one of the experienced children, and it was others who were new.

But the word was still too small; it meant nothing. Even *love* wasn't the right word. When Hal drove them in the El Dorado through the wild landscape each weekend, Alice was almost sickened by it all. She felt opened up and seared. Surely she'd seen such beauty before, because Rosalind kept saying how like the Azores this was, and even, in places, how like Australia. But if Alice had seen such beauty she hadn't been ready, she hadn't been able *really* to see it, and now all at once she was ripped open: all that light and color poured into her. It could not be encompassed by words such as *love* or *like;* it was moving and growing and green and live, even the ground smoking, steaming. What she could believe least of all was the way the land, dense with sugarcane and bananas and cornfields, with cactuses and aloes and palms, folded and heaved and suddenly threw up a peak, perfect like Cotopaxi, or jagged and sharp like Cayambe, white snow against blue, glimpsed through banana leaves or huge philodendra.

What with the blinding excursions and the parties and hot breathing under blankets, what with the squeezing curious little hands and the lips, and the skin that was warm and smelled of sand, everything around her all at once could be seen and felt and tasted. At night in the darkness of her bedroom it still burned within her eyelids, her hands and bare legs tingling with the feel of skin and trunks and rock.

How could grass grow so silky and deep, up to her knees, waving and liquid as water? How could she grasp what she saw? Flying was what she wanted; it burned her, a childish thing to want, unbearable. To coast and soar over all of it, to possess it that way, have it all in her eyes. Flying or eating, she didn't know what, there must be some way to *have* it.

¿Paraíso, no?

But it's a difficult thing to crave like this, land, especially when your body is so small. And a dangerous thing, too, when you have no business being there, when it's not even where you're from.

"So THE MAN IS actually keeping it up," said Hal at dinner a week later. "They've seized another boat. That brings it to five. Hundreds of thousands of dollars in fines."

"But surely," said Rosalind, "it *is* their water."

They paused as Carlita came in to pour wine. Alice could see how she kept her left hand clenched behind her back, and Alice looked at her but Carlita looked quickly away.

"I mean," said Rosalind, when Carlita had gone, "surely they have the right to control the fishing off their own coast."

"Sure," said Hal, "if you happen to think they have the right to invoke a law they alone imposed upon international waters. Two hundred miles, for Christ's sake. No one respects the two-hundred-nautical-mile law. Twelve miles is what's followed."

"But it is a law, then?"

"What?"

"Two hundred miles?"

"For God's sake, Rosalind. What I'm saying is that it's

not a law if it's not recognized. Which it isn't. It's their own self-made law. It's just a means," he said, "to bait us."

She laughed.

He stared at her.

"Well, it's funny," she said, cutting her steak. "Baiting. Fishing."

"Funny or not, it's giving the man clout. But we've been through all this before."

"Well I don't know then," she said. "What about our party? It hardly seems a good idea now."

"Sure it is. All the more so. Exactly what we're here for."

"REMEMBER," the students at the Académia were told in an assembly that was specially called when the sixth boat had been seized, "we are guests in this country. Whether you are here because your father is with the foreign service or with USAID or with the oil companies, we are still guests. You must be *careful*," the principal said, "not to be insulting. You must not call our Ecuadorian friends 'Eckies.' And never," he went on, shutting his eyes, "never call the Ecuadorians 'Ickies.'"

"But they are," muttered Dexter.

"Pardon?"

"I mean," he said, "they don't like us either."

"Could be," said Mr. Peterson from across the room, "they have their reasons."

IN CLOSETS in houses within gardens within spiked walls, the children kissed more than ever. Alice, too; everything was suddenly so hectic and hot. Desperate notes darted around the classrooms, passed from one damp hand to another, proclaiming love, hatred, revenge. Private rendezvous were arranged on Sunday afternoons outside the Hotel Quito.

Alice had one. She told Rosalind she was going to look at the bread-dough dolls at Folklórico, but instead, when the gate clanged behind her, she walked quickly the other way. She met Mark near the hotel, by a palm tree.

"Here," he said. His hair was white-blond and hung in his eyes, and out there with cars whizzing by he seemed smaller than at school. He handed her something in a box, in tissue, and looked away as she unwrapped it.

It was a ring, a complicated flower made of interwoven silver threads.

"Thanks," she said. She slid it on her finger, and they both looked at it on her hand. But for some reason the kissing didn't happen in daylight, outside in the world. She moved her fingers and examined the ring, and they looked at each other, and then he ran away.

But in locked pink bedrooms, in closets, in basements, hairless little bodies kissed passionately, frantic now because it was nearly summer and their time was almost up.

WHEN THE SEVENTH BOAT had been seized, Mr. Peterson pinned pictures of fish beside the map of Ecuador.

"The tuna fish," he said, "particularly enjoys swimming in the cool Humboldt current, along with the Pacific sailfish and marlin. Now here, this is the yellowfin tuna. It lives up to seven years and swims huge distances very fast, teaming up with dolphins. And this is the stripe-bellied bonito, look at the stripes on the belly, the silvery flanks. It swims a little higher in the ocean and doesn't mix with dolphins, which isn't smart because it gets caught more. This is the tuna you find in cans. Starkist, Bumblebee, Chicken of the Sea."

"Ask any mermaid you happen to see," sang Dexter, *"what's the best tuna—"*

The children drew the fish, the pectoral fins, the blue

backs, the dark stripes. Digestive system, nervous system; Alice labored over the colors of the scales and eye.

"Excellent drawings," said Hal when he saw them. "Good girl."

But to Rosalind, later, through the closet, he said, "Just what is this guy's point?"

Rosalind was standing by the mirror, trying to zip up her dress. "What?"

"Why teach the kids about tuna fish?"

"Well why not? Perhaps he thinks they ought to know what's causing all the fuss."

"It's hardly the life cycle of the damned fish."

"Oh for heaven's sake," she said, crouching down for shoes. "It's just a teaching opportunity. He's just trying to be current."

THE DAY OF THE Forders' big party, Ecuadorian gunships fired warning shots across the bow of an American boat.

"He's really pushing it," said Hal. "It was a freighter six hundred miles out to sea. *Six hundred miles.*" He shook his head. "But you can't call them stupid. It was two hundred miles from the Galápagos, so if you follow their screwy logic . . . Unbelievable balls."

"So what are we doing?"

"Well aside from demanding an apology we sure as hell are cutting our aid. They've dismissed our military advisers, so you can bet we'll take out the military group altogether."

"Which is—?"

"Which is," said Hal, "and I wish to God you'd learn some of this, what do you and the other wives talk about? Which is the group that's been in place since after the war, a group centralizing the Ecuadorians' own military. A lot of our money, matériel, goes into it."

"But surely," said Rosalind, "we get something for that?"

Hal laughed. "You bet we do. But they'll lose more than we do when we take it all back."

BEFORE THE PARTY, Hal paced around the house. He inspected glasses and bottles and with a gesture sent Carlita back to the kitchen to find more cocktail napkins. Rosalind had cut flowers in the garden and then poked stem after stem into the green spiked base at the bottom of a bowl until she'd created a fantastic explosion of color for the entrance hall. She'd spent hours perspiring with Maria in the kitchen, not only drawing up the initial menu but then showing her how to make a spicy cheese puff that had always been a hit.

"You come down, too, Alice," said Hal, "and say hello. Show off a little. Speak some Spanish."

¿Cómo está usted?

The party began. Manuel, in a short white jacket with a black bow tie, raced back and forth between the front door, where he clicked open the gate, and the second kitchen, where he retrieved the drinks tray. People came up the stone walkway and exclaimed at the extravagant flowers in the entrance hall.

"¡Qué lindo! ¡Qué bonito!"

Alice watched the parade of silver and orange and black clothes, slick or puffed or teased hair, frosted lipstick, frosted nails. Perfume floated up the stairs. Beyond the flowers hung the portrait of President Nixon.

"What would you like? What can I get you?" asked Hal, rubbing his hands as he greeted everyone. "Ah, Manuel, *gracias.*"

Hal glided around, sharp and alert as he spoke with the white-haired ambassador, then more confidential with high-heeled women, whispering into their hair things that made them laugh and look at him reproachfully as he stepped away again, pleased. Rosalind, leggy in a short dress, spoke gaily to men with black mustaches and gleaming bronze heads. Carlita ran back and forth through the swinging doors with trays, her eyes like the eyes of a deer; Alice glimpsed Maria through the door, hurrying to prepare the next tray. Herb Alpert and the Tijuana Brass filled the air, and Hal strode over now and then to crouch and select a new record.

When no one was in the entranceway Alice slipped downstairs and into the kitchen. Maria was finishing the cheese puffs, placing the last ones on the final tray in a series that ran along all the counters. She crossed herself and collapsed in a chair, the collar of her pale blue dress stained dark, her head with the wiry gray bun flung back and her gold fillings showing. She was the oldest, she would go to bed soon, but Carlita and Manuel would work until the end. Alice sat with Maria for a time, eating puffs and kneading the old woman's hands as together they watched the soap opera, a pink-suited lady with dyed blond hair, sobbing.

MEANWHILE, at a party for children up in the hills, the father of the little boy hosting the party, a father who was a tall marine, went to see how the kids were doing. There was dancing and music, and the lights were low. Children everywhere giggled when he came in, and he didn't at first switch on a light. But he noticed on one of the sofas a blanket that seemed to be moving. He looked at it a moment, then stepped closer, pulled it away, and stared down in disbelief at a peachy tangle of bare limbs.

"Like maggots," he would say later. "What the *fuck*?"

And the children themselves were stunned. Not just the two who were caught, but all of them. As if the instant the blanket was pulled up, they woke from a spell and found themselves transformed into something fetid.

The story would spread through the embassy the next day, from the marines at the gate and then up through the ranks (the girl's father was the number-three man). The attachés and ambassador and their wives all laughed, but secretly they were repelled, and there would be no more such parties for children.

In the Forder dining room the morning after the party, Rosalind sat shading her eyes at the table. Hal paced in and out of the bars of light that fell across the room.

"'Olga, do you fish?'" he said. "'Olga, do you fish?' I can't understand how you could have said that. The name of the *woman* is Olga Fisch. What you say when you offer a cigarette, Rosalind, is, 'Olga, do you smoke?' Not 'Olga, do you fish?' Of all things, fish. Christ almighty."

6

*A*FTER THAT THE tuna crisis subsided as the fish them-selves might, gliding deep. Velasco, Hal said, had slipped up. He had tried to oust someone high in the military, but had failed; his nephew, Acosta, had not been able to do it.

"I told you," Hal said. "Acosta's weak. Now he's been forced out, so Velasco's lost his main military support. It just goes to show the danger of a weak base."

"And?"

"Who knows. My guess is it'll be quiet. For a time."

WHICH IT WAS. Overhead, the Braniffs soared, each day tak-ing a fourth grader whose father's post was up. Michelle left, and Mark would soon, and so would Candi. Each to a dif-ferent part of the globe, foreign places the children only vaguely pictured and could not even spell with confidence. The little social constellations began to collapse, leaving lonely black holes.

"It's always harder for the ones staying behind than the ones leaving, isn't it," said Rosalind to Candi's mother, both of them smoothing the hair of their daughters as the girls wept and clutched at the airport.

Promises were made, as always.

"You have to write!" Candi sobbed to Alice.

"I will!"

"I won't ever forget you!"

"Yes you will!"

Noses and eyes streaming, Alice and Candi swore that they would both stare at the moon each night it was full and think *hard* about the other, so hard that surely space and time would dissolve.

Only later, after Candi had disappeared down the gangway with one last look through her tortoiseshell glasses, and after Alice had stood beneath the mosaic mural with her hands flat on the big glass window, staring until the orange Braniff had taxied, lifted, and disappeared in the sky, as Rosalind was driving her back home, reaching over now and then to squeeze her hand, did Alice realize, with a familiar, dull despair, that they had forgotten about the time zones. Because if she stared hard at the moon when it was full here, way on the other side of the world the sun would be shining for Candi. So it would never work, Candi was lost. Everyone was always lost. And letters really didn't do much.

WITH SCHOOL OVER and everyone gone, everything felt hollow. When she'd spent the night with Candi, at dinner the family would bow their heads and say grace, while Alice looked down at her plate. In bed now one night, she stared into the darkness and tried to do it. She thought hard to someone, to God, and imagined him somewhere, listening.

"Dear God," she tried. But it was silent, and everything

seemed empty all around. She didn't feel a thing. It was difficult not to think that her thoughts weren't just floating around in her own head, going nowhere.

Outside, the stars drifted in their imaginary patterns across the sky. In the Pacific, tunas and marlins swam their watery routes, changing direction in unison, flashes of silver in the dark. And deep underground, beneath Pichincha and Chimborazo, the fiery blood flowed in long, linking rivers.

In the empty days and weeks that followed, Alice pulled on her jeans patched with orange cats, slipped her glass beads from Miami International over her dirty-blond head, rubbed her hands on her shirt, and wandered around the house.

"Soon there will be all new friends," said Rosalind. She took Alice's hands and smiled, hopeful. "When school starts again and things get going."

But they never lasted, it never worked, and Alice did not have the heart.

In her room she looked at her things, at the old stuffed kangaroo Grandma Vi had given her, sitting on the dresser by the mirror. She went over to it and stood with it in her arms. The fur was soft, and had probably been a real kangaroo's, once. Little black plastic eyes and nose, a stiff tail. She looked at it reflected in her arms, and at her own face, the green eyes close together, hair lank at her cheeks, troubled mouth. She looked at the stuffed kangaroo, and put it back on the dresser. It was nice, but it was for children.

She wandered downstairs, over the polished floors, strumming her fingers on the windows' iron bars; she went into the kitchen. She helped Maria make bread, kneading the white dough as Maria muttered. She went into the garden and squatted near José as he pulled up weeds. He nodded to her but never spoke, his face creased and impenetrable beneath the hat. And Manuel's eyes were always shuttered when Hal and Rosalind weren't there; he never looked at Alice. Carlita moved nervously around her, giggling, trying to make her sneakers not squeak, as if the Forders and their race were unpredictable animals that should not be roused. Back in the kitchen, even though Maria offered a lap as soft as bread and let Alice press her face into her warm wrinkled neck, it was only kindness, the same as Maria would give the next girl who lived there when Alice was gone. Because who could afford or bother, when it was always so brief?

She went into the reception room. The feel of the brown sofa's rough fabric was comforting, the faint whiff it still held of Washington, and elsewhere. She sat there and took the whale tooth and held it, shut her eyes with it heavy and cold in her hand, and again pictured the tooth inside the mouth of a whale gliding deep in the sea.

She got up and went back outside, out to the sinking grass and the tossing fronds of the palm trees. The air was as electric as that blue sky looked, the white peak of Pichincha unreachable.

It was comforting, though, the mountain. Illusory, yet always there.

"You can climb it, you know," Mr. Peterson had told her in May, when he found her gazing up at it from the volleyball court. "You don't have to just stand there and stare at Pichincha. There it is! When school starts, I'll be going up with two of the boys. Want to come?"

"I'll tell you something," said Hal, drumming his fingers on the dining-room table as they waited for Carlita to clear. "It may seem quiet now, but Velasco has made some very important people very unhappy. These things don't just go away.

And it sure as hell doesn't help that Castro's coming to visit him. Castro! Not much question how they'll vote on Taiwan." He raised his eyebrows. "And where does that put us? Nineteen sixty-one all over again."

THE BRANIFFS came and went, stray dogs wandered in the streets, Maria baked cinnamon bread on Saturdays while Hal and Rosalind played tennis. Before school started, Mr. Peterson took Alice and two boys, Theo and Sammy, into the old part of town on a local bus. They walked through what seemed to be walls in churches and along crooked cobblestone streets. People were selling things from stalls on both sides in the dark, and the air was full of smoke and voices, chickens scurrying around everyone's feet. From a stall in a corner they bought boots like Mr. Peterson's, made of tough raw leather.

"You'll have to carry a backpack," he said, "but you can use an old one of mine. I'll bring the food, and the boys can carry water. Wear those boots every day until they're softened up. And practice walking with the backpack, too, because you'll need to balance."

MR. GOODBARS AND cornflakes arrived at the commissary; Doctor Knobloch gave gamma globulin shots; in quiet rooms, foreign-service officers pored over the latest infant mortality rates; oil companies began building the pipeline. The diplomatic pouch flew in each week; in Bolivia the Quichuans were removed from their land; on Saturdays the embassy showed *Mary Poppins* and *Born Free*. Out at the haciendas, in the heaving green landscape, American men taunted heifers with red capes, while outside the bullring the women dissolved in laughter and reached down for their drinks. Alice walked around and around the block in her new boots until she got blisters, and then she walked even more until the blisters calloused over.

Then the sleek buses were zooming through the city, and school began again. All new children all over again. Smoke rose slowly from Pichincha.

WE MUST REMIND YOU, especially those who are new, never to drink the water.

But they weren't warned about the flowers, and a little girl who had only just come ate a long trumpet-shaped flower and hallucinated for thirty-two hours. A very little girl, she couldn't have known; the flower was pale orange and smelled overpoweringly sweet. She only nibbled the edges.

Then the story went around about how Ms. Barkin, the new English teacher, had gone by herself to the Amazon. A long, greenish woman with lank red hair and watery eyes, she'd taken local buses and hitchhiked. She was gone for several weeks. When she came back she looked as though there, in the jungle, she had sunk her body into all the vegetation, the living insects and fetid blossoms and rot, and that even though she had been there so long, all by herself in the jungle, she still had not had enough of it; even though things may have crawled in and out of her body, under her toenails and into her mouth and nostrils and secret openings, in her eyes was an insatiability, like a drug.

"WHERE THE HELL do they get these teachers?" said Hal. He was taking his tie off in quick swoops as Alice watched from the perch in her closet, where she read with a flashlight.

"That teacher going native," he said, "that one with the poncho and beard and Cuenca sandals. The one taking Alice up Pichincha. Where's he from?"

"New Hampshire, I think he said." Rosalind unbuttoned

her blouse but didn't take it off, just kept sitting on the bed, staring out the balcony doors. The way she sat her stomach bulged a little over the panty hose, and she let her feet dangle.

"New Hampshire." Hal came to the closet in his shirt.

"He's just very keen about the country," said Rosalind.

"And why not. Explore the country, buy the bread dolls, climb goddamned Chimborazo if you want. But don't go over that line."

"Which line?"

Hal turned to look at her, the back of his head three feet from Alice.

"I don't see that it matters so much," said Rosalind. "If you go over that line. Which line, anyway? I don't see how it matters."

"It matters, Rosalind, if you are trying to negotiate. You cannot negotiate if you look like a fool, if you look like you don't know who the hell you are, or where the hell you come from. It's a matter of weakness, Rosalind."

"Well he's not negotiating, he's a teacher, and Alice likes him very much."

ON A SATURDAY MORNING, Rosalind drove Alice along the road that zigzagged up Pichincha. They went past grand houses and then crumbling huts until all those fell away, past the tennis courts, up through fields until the fields ended, and higher until the road finally stopped, and there was nothing but mountainside, bare. When they got out of the car it was dizzying to look down at the city, to be so high.

"Better tie those boots tight," Hal had said as Alice sat on the front steps lacing them. "Double knots. Like this." He crouched before her and demonstrated, and sunburned skin showed through the hair thinning at the top of his head. He stood and looked down at her with his hands on his hips.

"Don't want to step on a lace and lose your balance all the way up there, now do you," he'd said, before tossing Rosalind the car keys.

Mr. Peterson and Theo and Sammy were already there. Everyone wriggled into their backpacks.

"It'll be fine," Mr. Peterson said to Rosalind, who stood there with her hands clasped. "We've done this a dozen times."

From here the city was so small, just a little bigger than Alice's hand when she held it before her and shut one eye.

Rosalind shielded her eyes and walked to the edge of the earthen plateau. She stood gazing down, and Alice looked at her mother, standing there in a pale dress and sandals against vast folds of ancient land.

"Doesn't it all look small," said Rosalind. "There's the embassy. Somewhere's the house." She stood a moment longer, then came over to Alice, and hugged her tight. "Why am I letting you do this," she whispered.

"She'll be fine," said Mr. Peterson. "A born mountaineer."

"Yes," said Rosalind. "Well. Home safe tomorrow by six."

Mr. Peterson put up his hand to promise, and she waved to everyone, got in the convertible, and wound slowly back down the road.

When the car had disappeared, it was quiet. You could not see anyone anywhere. The city was too far away to really believe that anyone was down there. The clouds seemed heavy and near.

"Ready?" said Mr. Peterson. They put their backs to the city and began. He walked with a stick, his bright hair and beard curling beneath a striped cap.

Up there the ground was like the back of a giant bull, smooth and sloping away on either side, the grass as thin as hair on a hide. The trail had been made by snow that sometimes covered the peak and then melted, running down the mountain. In places the trail was barely visible, where the water must have traveled in sheets, but sometimes it had been gouged deep by a torrent, pebbles loose on either side.

"Thin air," said Mr. Peterson. He stopped and took a deep breath. "Have to be careful. Easy to get dizzy."

As they rose along the huge back, on either side grew round clumps of plants that looked like urchins, something you'd find in the sea. One was springy when Alice sat on it, but made of tiny tough leaves and blossoms.

They camped at dusk in a saddle of meadow at the base of the rock peak, which they would climb the next day. It seemed to drift even faster against the sky, to topple upon them, now that it rose so close. There had been almost no sound all day, just a huge pleated surface of land thousands of feet up, beneath a slowly moving sky. Crests of mountain stretching off in every direction were lit pink and coral as the sun set. And at night the stars were fathoms deep, so bright they cast shadows. In the tent, in her sleeping bag, Alice's hair smelled of smoke.

The next day they left their gear behind in the tents and began to climb the peak. Without packs it was easier, just bare hands clutching rock, and boots wedging into niches. Alice was finally used to how the mountain kept falling, how when you clung to it with hands and knees it seemed you were riding something across the sky. She concentrated on each place to grip and each crack to jam the toe of her boot. They rose slowly, losing their breath and pausing often, the four of them clinging to the stone in the sky. When she looked down once, the tents were tiny, the air so clear she could reach down and flick them over. Then suddenly the tents, the brown flanks they'd climbed the day before—all of it was gone, there was nothing but white mist. She could just see Mr. Peterson's face, drops of dew on his beard.

"Clouds," he said, fog swirling around him.

Then they passed through the clouds to another world. The sky was saturated blue, so dense it was unbearable that you couldn't just clutch it. And beneath was no ground, nothing but a soft white blanket of cloud rolling to the horizon, with icy white peaks of the Andes jutting through. It truly seemed that there was nothing beneath them, as if once you got this high you no longer had anything to do with the world far beneath you, because all that was real was this white sea of mountain and cloud.

They rested for a time, leaning against the rock, eating peanuts and chocolate. Mr. Peterson checked everyone's bootlaces.

"El Paso de la Muerte next," he said. "And that's what we have to worry about. We'll use ropes."

"El Paso de la Muerte," yodeled Theo, who had done the climb before. His voice disappeared in the cool vapor.

The pass was a long ribbon of rock stretching between two precipices; it was just wide enough to walk upon, like a gangplank, but at either side it dropped away, sheer.

Everyone got attached to a rope, and one by one they crossed. The boys went first. Theo walked calmly, arms out at either side for balance; Sammy scrambled over on hands and knees, whispering. Alice would go next, Mr. Peterson behind her.

"Nothing to worry about, we've got you with the rope."

It was a short walk, really. On either side, it seemed actually to drop away into nothing because of the clouds and mist. And if she could not see the drop, it was not really there. So Alice just walked, arms out at either side, feet dipping as if on the balance beam.

Then Mr. Peterson joined them, and they were on the other side, home free.

It was silent there, lifeless, a landscape of rock and sand, lunar. Just the scuffing of their boots in the pumice, their breaths in the unknown cold air.

"There it is," said Mr. Peterson, pointing to a jagged boulder. "The top. Alexander von Humboldt stood somewhere around here. Although it's erupted since his time."

So Alice climbed this last rock, clinging with hands and knees, to the tip. There she clutched the stone and looked into the mist, and tried to believe that she was at that highest point of rock she'd watched sailing across the sky.

To GET BACK DOWN they ran. Right down the wide dry river that from Quito you could see sometimes was snow, but now was a flow of powdered pumice. It was like a sand dune in the sky, but it went on and on, down into the clouds. The four of them gripped hands and ran, and it was soft as they stumbled, plunged, lost their footing, fell, and were dragged laughing by the others to their knees again. It had once been stone, and liquid, and fire, it had been everything and now was powder. Alice tore free from the others and ran alone, down the mountainside in the middle of the sky. She was so light she could almost fly, falling, rolling, staggering on her knees, until she could no longer breathe, her mouth and hair full of powder, ecstatic.

AFTERWARD, AFTER THEY trudged down the sloping hide and the city came into view, and gradually grew larger and more real until at last, somehow, they stepped into it again, what she had seen still burned in Alice's eyes. And in her hands, too; they still felt that stone fifteen thousand feet up, stone that had scarcely been touched or seen, raw, original stone. That pumice that had blown as red liquid from the hot inner earth, and flowed and then dried and dissolved to fine sand, it was still in her hair, in her mouth, in her skin.

Hal laughed when Manuel let her in that night and she stood, bleached and blasted, in the entrance hall. "Look at that," he said. "The explorer returns."

"Into the tub," said Rosalind. "Then tell us all about it."

So up Alice went, legs aching, head dazzled, up the implausible stairs. In the bathtub she slid under the warm water. She opened her eyes and let herself bob, thin bones bumping on porcelain, hair floating like seaweed. Bubbles tumbled from her nose, and snow turned into rivers, and rivers turned into trails, and maybe she could turn into something else, too: just breathe in, breathe this water in deeply, open her mouth and be a fish, and slip away from this particular world, swim in hot underground currents.

7

THE SCHOOL BUSES zoomed around the city each morning, the embassy men took their different routes to work, but Velasco Ibarra seemed to be waiting again, before making another move. It was quiet, yet as if things were happening underground that up in the sun you couldn't see. The Académia children did their homework and played soccer against the local teams, kicking and being kicked hard in the shins. In the embassy an attaché reviewed the newest figures on illiterate girls. In New York, Ecuador cast the wrong vote on Taiwan. In the garden of an oil family, a green caterpillar with vivid yellow stripes clung to a hydrangea stem, eating, its body soft but fringed with spines that would paralyze a curious child who touched it. In the empty kitchen of another house, a large spider, furred like a mammal, crawled across terra-cotta tiles and disappeared inside a cabinet.

And down from Quito, down the muddy mountain roads, through wet banana plantations and over the hot sugarcane coast, far out in the Pacific, bigeye tuna were swimming in schools. A sheening mass raced at different depths, following the cool current of water, which once had been known only to them until it was charted by Alexander von Humboldt. The ocean was roomier now than it had been in his time; there were noticeably fewer fish. Travelers in those days had remarked upon the flying fish that landed on deck, and the albatross that was so easily shot, and its strange cry, its clumsiness as it fell.

Over in the Oriente, far underground, beneath the palms and yucca that stuck up all over the wild green surface, lay deep silent seas of oil. Oil that had once been living plants and creatures, until millions of years of earth crushed and transformed them.

"You know some kids in oil, don't you, Alice?" asked Hal at the dining-room table. "The Académia must be full of them."

BY THIS TIME the pipeline and the Pan-American Highway were well on their way. To Alice and other Académia children, the Pan-American Highway had something to do with the Panama hats. It was just that the Panama hats were actually made in Ecuador, and were therefore (like the highway) connected to both countries, which themselves (they learned) had once been joined, when Simón Bolívar was alive, and all Latin America rose up against Spain. These things dwelled in their fifth-grade brains, things to learn, things that changed, confusing. Just as South America had once not been joined to North America, there had been no Panama, and South America was alone in the sea, an island floating like Australia.

"Lonely continents," said Mr. Peterson. "Lonely continents, drifting. Imagine that, the continents moving around.

And the animals that used to live here! The glyptodon, the mylodon, the giant sloths: wonderful, strange, strange creatures. That sloth," he said, holding up a lifelike rendering of the sloth when alive, "was so very slow that lichen grew in its fur. But then one day the saber-toothed tiger came down from the north, once it could walk across Panama."

THE RAW NEW HIGHWAY cut through banana plantations, cornfields, and plains dotted with cactuses like green coral, Cotopaxi perfect and snowy in the distance. As it rolled through the gum trees, the new oil pipeline snaked toward Esmeraldas, where runaway African slaves had once settled, and beyond Esmeraldas, to the sea. The pipe pushed through jungle, and trees no one had ever seen crashed down before it; it rode along high, lonely ridges.

"Boom time," said Hal, as he had said once before.

"Ravaging," said Mr. Peterson, showing the course of the pipeline on a map.

"A *lot* of money about to pour into the country," said Hal. "We'll see," he said. "We'll just see."

NOW THAT THE Académia children no longer danced or kissed in closets, they had ordinary slumber parties. Girls gathered in houses behind stone walls and told stories, did crafts, did cartwheels.

A girl named Claire who liked to stay inside and make things—candles with layers of different-colored wax, scarves with bands of different-colored wool—looked up from her macramé at a slumber party one night. There had been a scream far away in the city.

"Rape," she said, and returned to her doily.

"The thing to do not to get raped," said another girl, "is just act like you're crazy."

She stood up and demonstrated: strawberry-blond hair falling in her face, strawberry-pink tongue lolling from her mouth, she limped through the reception room, lurching crazily from side to side, like the boy with one leg longer than the other.

THEN ONE OF THE girls at the Académia was trampled to death by a horse. She had either been thrown or had fallen, it wasn't clear, and none of the children could ask as the news was given in an assembly, all of them staring straight ahead, sick. But once she had fallen she simply lay stunned in the long grass, as the horse, in a panic, reins tangled around its legs, reared up, stumbled backward, then forward again, and once more backward, and did not know what to do, while she lay there beneath it, until her bones had been broken, she had been trampled into the watery grass, her blood running into the rich soil, the mud.

FINALLY, in November, Velasco Ibarra did it again.

"What did I tell you," said Hal.

First one boat was seized, then another. The Ecuadorians took the American boats the way the American boats took the tuna. Hal paced in the reception room, from the fireplace to the barred window and back.

"Peru all over again," he said as he went to answer the phone. "Nineteen sixty-three all over again."

ON NEW YEAR'S EVE, a general with a glass of champagne in his hand made a toast to Presidente Velasco Ibarra. In the name of all the Ecuadorian armed forces, he swore perpetual loyalty.

"DON'T BELIEVE IT for a second," said Hal. "Velasco doesn't have a chance in the elections. And I tell you, the fellow

likely to win, that Guayaquileño peddler—some very important people are not happy with him. And with those oil concessions about to come in? Bolivia," he said, "is not a nice
example."

"I CAN'T HELP asking myself about all of this," said Rosalind
to Mrs. Bachrach and Mrs. O'Donnell, who had come over
for lunch. By this time there were American sanctions
against the country.

"Do we really have any right?" she said. "Not just with
those damned fish, God knows. To be here altogether, you
know what I mean. To be *involved* in all of this. I don't know.
Do we really belong here?"

"SO WHERE WOULD you like to be, Rosalind?" Hal said
through the closet. "Is there a place you would rather be?"

"Oh stop it. I don't know. I just don't understand who
has a right to be where."

"It's not a matter of a right, it's a matter of responsibility."

"A responsibility to take what's under other people's
feet?"

"What are you talking about, Rosalind. Oil? If they didn't
even know what was under their feet, then, sure. We help
them develop. That's what we're here for. How else will this
country get out of the Stone Age?"

"I don't see how that's just," she said.

"What's not just? They're getting plenty of money for
that oil. And money is something they need."

"But aren't there other things, more *important* things?"

"Oh for Christ's sake, Rosalind," said Hal.

THEN ALL AT ONCE it was Carnival again. Balloons flew
through the streets as the bus zoomed the children home.

But this year Alice was prepared, having bought balloons at La Favorita.

Once she got home—and had hopped hysterically while she waited for Manuel to open the gate, but he stood more inside the door than out, shielding his head—she ran straight to the bathroom to fill the balloons. Then, with them jiggling in a bucket, she hurried to her balcony, opened the door as little as possible, ducked, and crawled out to the end. In bursts she jumped up and threw at anything moving down on the street. Old women begging. The men outside the *bodega*. The limping boy who lived on the corner, who hopped in delight when he saw her and then disappeared and began to pelt balloons back. The windshields of passing cars.

Then she hit Hal by mistake, as he suddenly rounded a corner. There he was, before she'd seen who, the balloon already flying. Right on his chest, on his suit, on his shirt, on his tie, exploding in a splash on his long shocked face. She dropped to the floor of the balcony, gasping with laughter and terrified, as Hal buzzed and buzzed for Manuel to let him in.

BUT THE NEXT DAY, in the middle of all the yellow and purple balloons splatting against the school bus windows, suddenly there was a rock. From nowhere it cracked against the tinted glass, shattering.

"I told you," cried Dexter, who had been sitting closest and now stared at the shaky glass web.

Claire and the girl who'd eaten the flower started crying. The bus driver sped down Avenida Guayaquil.

"What did we ever do to *them*?"

THE CHILDREN had only been inside the compound of the Académia half an hour when military jeeps appeared. They lined up at the black iron gates, and the gates were hurriedly opened. Then men in uniform were jumping out, running through the buildings. Up the stairs, along the white walls, past the crayoned pictures of Bolivia and Peru. As the soldiers ran through the buildings with their heavy boots and machine guns, the children sat still at their desks.

Coup was the word that ran through the classrooms.

"Coup d'état," whispered the children.

After the soldiers had been through his room, Mr. Peterson stood trembling in his hiking boots and alpaca sweater, his pale eyes cold behind the glasses.

"No reason to be afraid," he said to the fifth graders. "Because my guess is that we and the military are on the same side. In overturning the government, I mean. They've come here to protect us."

THE CHILDREN were hurried into a hasty assembly. Yes, the military had taken over; Velasco Ibarra had been removed from office; the government had changed.

"Although there is no danger to us, the embassy is on full alert," said the principal. "The country is in an *estado de sitio*. We are to return to our homes at once."

The children lined up outside the buses and boarded. They were silent then, peering through the windows, hands and knees pressed together, as one by one the buses pulled out through the gates. No one was on Avenida de las Americas. There were no pregnant buses, no flying balloons, just dogs sniffing at the corners.

"WELL," SAID HAL that night, striding over the tasseled carpet. "That's that. Velasco Ibarra is out." He stopped and swirled his drink. "The end of the Quinto Velasquismo. Absolutely bloodless." He ran a hand over his head. His face looked hot.

"So now?" said Rosalind.

"A military junta."

"Junta." She wrapped her arms around herself and shivered in the gold chair. "Such a sinister word."

"Junta," Hal repeated, as if tasting, and nodded. "Three men, headed by Lara."

"And the elections?"

Hal laughed. "They've bypassed elections."

Rosalind nodded slowly.

"And?" she said after a moment.

"And what?" He glanced around, tapping his glass.

"And *us*?"

He shrugged. "We'll be fine. The locals are euphoric. You have to understand, Rosalind, a lot of money will be pouring into the country, and now at least it will be going the right way. The locals just couldn't be happier. They're calling this the *carnavalazo*."

"Yes," she said. She laughed a little and lifted her glass but let it hover before her. "What I meant, though," she said, and now her body seemed to contort, as if something were twisting her from the chair. "What I *meant*," she said, "is just how much were we involved?"

Hal regarded her. "As a matter of fact, Rosalind, we had nothing to do with it."

She stared at him and laughed. "How is that possible?"

He shrugged.

"How is that *possibly* possible?"

He didn't answer, and took a sip of his drink.

"We had nothing against it, though, did we," she said. "Nothing against bypassing elections."

He considered her again. "The locals," he repeated, "just couldn't be happier."

8

AFTER THE COUP there would be arrests, Hal said; corruption trials, the usual bloodletting. Alice looked for signs of bloodletting through the bus window. But everything seemed exactly the same, the city quiet and hot, with its winged white buildings and curlicue churches, barefoot boys herding cows along streets, the fields on Pichincha burning. On Saturdays the children screamed at Dracula in the embassy, and outside, high on a pole, the American flag slowly furled and unfurled against the primitive sky.

Soon after the coup, Hal would receive his new post; their time in Quito would be up. In his study he was already organizing his albums, whistling as he sorted through papers and files. Alice watched him from outside, through the barred den window, as she walked slowly past on the stone wall, placing her sneakered feet with precision between sharp pieces of glass.

Fresh bread on Saturdays as always; tennis. While Hal

and Rosalind put on their whites, Alice helped Maria roll out long soft snakes of dough. And far away, in the jungle or near the coastal plains, tropical trees were being cut down to make room for the highway and pipeline, and soil that was loosened by the removal of roots began to slide, great mud slides that covered villages completely, so that you wouldn't know anything had ever been there. Just as living things had once been covered by silt and over millions of years transformed, but now rose again, bubbled up warm and sometimes flaming, pure vaporous energy, inanimate life.

Rosalind wandered through the gleaming house in her little white dress. Her tennis shoes squeaked on the floors Manuel had waxed every Thursday they'd lived there and probably every Thursday before that. She tossed a green tennis ball back and forth between her hands; she stood at the barred windows and gazed out at the snapdragons growing by the high stone wall.

"So?" Alice heard her say as her feet squeaked behind Hal down the halls. "So what do you think, Hal. Tell me. Which lucky country will be getting us next?"

He didn't answer. There was never any answer, or no answer Alice could hear. He came through the swinging door to the kitchen in his tennis whites, his legs long and lean.

"If you're playing," he said to Alice, "get your things."

THE TENNIS COURTS were on wedges cut into Pichincha. Alice hit against the wall in one, while on the other side Rosalind and Hal played doubles with Tom Mueller and a man who was new.

Their sneakers squeaked upon the clay, faces burning red in the equatorial light. When Rosalind missed a volley, the others relaxed, suspended. Her little skirt flipped with each step as she went to pick up the balls.

Hal ran a hand over his head, leaned toward his partner, and said something. The new man pulled a face and laughed. Hal twirled the racket between his palms and smiled.

Across the court Rosalind was waiting to serve.

The wall at the edge of the courts angled up from the ground until it met the mountain, and there Pichincha resumed. The courts were just brief, raw indentations; it was easy to imagine mud sliding down, filling them. Alice climbed onto this wall that held the mountain back, then walked up it as it angled high above the courts, until the ground became pasture again. She stood there in the long grass against the sky, looking down at the others on the court below, the tiny green ball bouncing between them.

In the car on the way home the gum trees whipped by, and the clouds drifted slowly above. The smell of eucalyptus was strong. Rosalind turned to look at Hal, just as once, long ago, she had turned to ponder Rupert. She stretched her bare arm along the back of the seat, as she had once upon a time in Australia. Not her right arm as then, though, but her left, for everything was backward down there. Hal didn't look at her as he steered, as Rupert hadn't then, either. Rupert had a new post, somewhere Alice couldn't spell. A letter had come with a foreign stamp, which had an unreadable print that looked like smoke, like the cigarette smoke pluming from Hal's cigarette, drifting behind them into the sky.

"I JUST CAN'T understand," Hal said to Rosalind that night through the closet, "why you signed up for this life to begin with."

THAT WEEKEND, Rosalind and Alice drove down to the coast, as they'd always said they would, because it was now or never. An embassy group was camping at a beach near Salinas. Just women and children, Rosalind said, because what else were they supposed to do when the children had holidays and the men couldn't come? Or *wouldn't* come. Or at any rate, didn't. And anyway, things were back to normal; no more *estado de sitio;* it was fine. They could do whatever they liked.

This she said several times as she sped the car down the avenues of Quito, smacking the steering wheel for stress, then as she drove outside the city and through the potato fields, past the gum trees that someone sometime had brought there and planted, and weren't they, she said, a bloody long way from home.

Rosalind struggled with the car and you could hear it strain as they twisted and turned down the muddy mountain road, descending nine thousand feet. On the inner side, the mountain wall was loose with fallen rocks, and on the other side the slope dropped away. Sometimes the mist was so thick they couldn't see more than a few meters before them; sometimes the road wound through plantations, shrouded with long serrated leaves and bunches of green bananas with dangling red cords. Waterfalls thundered in gulches; rocks fell; sometimes it seemed only three wheels were on the road. The air grew warmer and damper the lower they went, and when they descended to the coastal plain, it was tropical. They didn't reach the shore until dark, their hair whipping in the hot humid wind. There were oil derricks and refineries near Salinas, and they belched orange flames, reflected in the slick black sea.

The group was camping among palm trees on the beach, where the sand was soft and cool. All the mothers had set up tents, each mother sharing with her children. Rosalind turned hers and Alice's to face the sea. Coconuts dripped milk from the bending palms, and occasionally one fell with a *tock.* Fires were lit, and the women roasted fish.

"Fresh from the sea," Mrs. Bachrach said. "The fishermen came in just before you got here. And you'll never guess what it is."

"Oh, no."

The women laughed and struck their beer bottles together, toasting as they roasted the fish.

"Tuna, tuna, *atún*," said one. "God, are we sick of you."

"And *them*."

"Our men?"

"Amen."

"Amen," said Rosalind. She shut her eyes and raised her bottle to the sky.

The others grew quiet. "So?" Mrs. O'Donnell asked her.

Rosalind let her arm fall. The women gathered together and spoke quietly.

THAT NIGHT Rosalind and Alice lay on their stomachs, chins on their crossed arms as they gazed out to sea. The listless waves glowed with lines of froth as they broke, and beyond those lines it was dark.

"Nothing but water," Rosalind said. "Nothing but water between us and home." She laughed a little in the darkness. "Maybe we'll just go," she said. "We could, you know. Just pack up and go." She propped her head on her elbow and looked at Alice. "You don't even remember home, do you."

But when Rosalind said it, there they were, the wattle, bottlebrush, snakes, and Banksia Man; the pebbled path beneath her feet, Grandma Vi with her thin freckled arms fanning herself with a palm frond. They all still dwelled inside Alice, near her ribs, like pain but not claimable, nothing. There was a new girl at the Académia who had lived in Australia, and she grew fierce when she spoke of it: it was *hers*.

And she was right. In her eyes Alice thought she could see that ghost country moving.

She stared out at the listless, moonlit sea sloshing between the continents. South America, Australia, Africa: anyone could see on the map what had happened, how the continents had split apart, wandered off.

Far away, at the bottom of the ocean, fire was pouring from a crack, pouring into the water like hot gushing gore. All along this beach, she knew, because Mr. Peterson had told them, all along this beach one whole piece of the surface of the earth was being forced under this very continent. Right under her body as she lay on the sand, a whole piece of the earth's crust was being jammed under, down to where it would melt. And it wasn't even very deep down where all that happened, where it was so hot that earth cracked and melted. Only forty miles or so, he said. Which you could easily drive in less than an hour. Which Hal could drive faster in the El Dorado. She could see it, the blue convertible speeding straight down, Hal's long fingers on the wheel.

Beside her, Rosalind sighed. She stretched out her arms, kissed Alice, and lowered the netting over the tent's opening.

THE NEXT MORNING was gray, and Alice and Rosalind got up before the others and walked along the beach, looking for shells. There were lots but they were mostly broken; scattered among them were devil's purses, jellyfish, long glassy worms. All over the sand were fragments of fish, heads and torn tails and fins. Alice found a dead dogfish like a baby shark, as long as her arm. Its eyes were dull, its pronged tail limp and scuffed with sand, its little crescent mouth fixed open. She nudged sand over to bury it, but then saw there were more, the beach was rich and rotting.

Farther down the beach a crowd had formed, people gathering excitedly around something. Several children ran from the group, their eyes fixed on what was cupped in their hands. Alice and Rosalind went down to see, and Alice slipped into the crowd, and through it. In the center a giant sea turtle lay on its back, a man with a knife scooping from its bloody belly.

When Alice pushed her way out, Rosalind was standing with her hand at her mouth. She grabbed Alice and they ran to the water.

"God," she said, on her knees, heaving, while Alice held back her hair. "Oh, but shit, they have to eat." She laughed a little and heaved again.

After a time she looked up at Alice, her chin and nose runny. "You know that, don't you? People have to *eat*."

She buckled again, but nothing came. She pushed sand over the vomit and knelt there, her head hanging and hands sinking in the wet sand. Frothy water lapped over her strong fingers, over the emerald in her ring, and drifted back again.

"I just want," she whispered, "to get *away*."

Down the beach, the man bent and rinsed his knife in the water, wiped it gently on his palm.

But had the turtle been coming or going back to sea when it was caught? Maybe her eggs were already planted safe in the sand?

AT THE END OF the week the women took down the tents and packed up, tanned and bleached and gritty. They hugged each other as if they had been through something. Then again Rosalind struggled with the car back up the mountain, a stream of exhaust floating among the green bananas.

When they were in the high lap of the Andes, back where the air was light and dry, she slowed down a little, by the eucalypt woods. The trees were skinny and tall, and their pink bark peeled away in strips from their smooth, bony trunks. Rosalind slowed the car more, looking past Alice and into the trees, as if she saw something among them. Her wrists rested at the top of the steering wheel.

Finally she stopped the car, not quite at the edge of the road. All around it was quiet. A breeze blew, the long dangling gum leaves flitting and turning, their smell dry and tart. Rosalind shut her eyes.

"But you know," she said, "I've given up our citizenship. They won't just let us come home."

9

School ended soon after, and then the house began to do what houses always did. But Alice could move through it and refuse to notice. The squares left on walls when pictures came down, the sound of her footsteps loud on the floor once the rugs had been rolled up. Soon this house would dissolve behind them, because nothing, nothing, ever stayed. Mr. Peterson was already gone.

She went to the front garden and lay facedown in the grass, and stared through the fine green jungle. From the earth beneath her head came a drumming. Down the soil sank, growing cooler, then it turned to clay, and then to stone, giving way at last to that burning blood. She opened her mouth and imagined eating the grass; she looked at her thin hand lying there. Her hand could just petrify. Skin could turn into rock and dissolve right here in the soil. She tunneled her hand deep into the grass, down into the moist roots, and held it there a time. She drew it out. Dirt was wedged under her nails and there were green stains on her fingers, but the hand was still hers, small and something she could feel, insignificant.

Running down Pichincha—it could have happened there. It should have. She could have just broken apart as she flew, crumbled like ash that once had been rock but now melted at a touch. Just break apart, turn into powder. Maybe even now she could hurl her body into the earth if she wanted, dissolve herself in it, forcibly. Because girls could sometimes do that, she knew this from books. They could become trees, or they could become stone, or rivers if they wanted. They could run as fast as possible and suddenly plunge into the earth, and underground they'd turn into liquid, and flow.

In the museum where the fourth graders went on a field trip a little boy sat on display in a glass box, a dead Indian prince. He'd been dug up from his burial place somewhere high in the Andes. A little boy, maybe seven: Alice had stared through the glass at him. His small brown hand was shriveled so that you could see the bones through his papery skin, and his head had dropped upon his birdlike chest, as if he'd just fallen asleep. He was dressed, wrapped in cloths, but he somehow seemed naked, alone and surrounded by glass. Across from Alice, Dexter had tapped at the glass, as if to stir him. Surely the boy wished he was where he belonged, alone in his quiet deep ground.

Alice rolled over slowly, spread out her arms and legs, and shut her eyes. Then she opened them and stared up at the deep, blinding blue. Was the sky hot or cold? The windows of jets against your forehead were always cold. But right now it was easy to imagine the sky hot. An infernally hot, burning sky. A sky that, were you up there flying, would melt you, incinerate you, and you wouldn't even fall because there'd be nothing left, you'd be nothing but ash. But even if it was cold, you'd dissolve: you'd be so cold you'd petrify and shatter.

THROUGH THE WALLS, through the closet, through the swinging kitchen door, came Hal's and Rosalind's voices. Alice didn't listen to the words, though. They didn't make any difference.

At night she lay in bed and stared through the ceiling to those stars, that sky; she stared down, through the mattress and the floor and the ground, straight through the earth, to where everything flowed hot.

If she wanted something hard enough, maybe it could happen?

She lay there with her dirty-blond head on the pillow, on the pillowcase that Carlita had washed and hung in the sun and ironed and folded and then put on her bed, her dirty-blond head that could explode.

HAL'S AND ROSALIND'S voices flew through the house, along the gleaming hallways and even through the barred windows; or else there were silences. And all the time the house was shedding them. The black leather table was no longer there; the whale tooth was already gone. Carlita moved about silently as the house emptied; Manuel still buffed the banister.

When Alice found Manuel late one afternoon with his collar undone in the kitchen, and asked to be let out, he did not say a word but went to the button that opened the electric gate. She walked past the pineapple palm, the lemon tree, the snapdragons in their row, and when she reached the gate, Manuel let it swing open.

THE STREET SMELLED of urine, as always, and burning corn. By the *bodega* the men glanced up when the gate shut behind her. She walked around the walled, glass-spiked corner, down the street to the avenue where pregnant buses tore along and were caught by men as if they were bulls, and where she'd once seen a dog hit by a car, and then hit again as it tried to crawl to the curb. A man stood in a corner on Seis de Diciembre with his ponchoed back turned, a dark stain growing on the sidewalk just before him; boys shouted *¡Chiclé! ¡Chiclé!* and shook their boxes; a woman with braids and a black hat squatted by a fire, frying plantains and kernels of corn as big as horses' teeth.

In the ocean there were rip currents and bull sharks. In the jungle were jaguars, electric eels, and pythons. An American boy had been kidnapped and shot in Bolivia, or maybe Peru, while his family was there on holiday. Since his brain was already dead by the time his parents got him, they decided to donate his parts to hospitals all over the country. So there they flew, in all directions, his liver, his kidney, his heart.

On this very street, Seis de Diciembre, Dexter told Alice he'd once seen a man decapitated by a bus. It sped by fast and there must have been a piece of metal or something sticking out, because the next thing you knew the man lay there, gushing, his head rolling away.

The Mayas cut off heads and strung them on a rope. Or maybe it was the Aztecs. And they cut off heads and threw them into the ground to help the potatoes and corn grow.

Alice walked up the Avenida Guayaquil. Lights came on in some buildings as real light drained from the sky. Buses rattled by, cars honked at corners, but no one noticed her, she was small. And after a time she knew that she could walk and walk but nothing would happen, what she wanted would not happen, the earth would not crack open at her feet and take her.

She had all her sucres in her pocket. It had seemed like

the thing to do, bring them. They'd be worthless again soon, anyway. On the street, women sold pieces of sugarcane, pineapple slices of coconut lying in water, and popsicles they pulled from big trash cans.

"*Dos, por favor.*"

"*¿Dos?*"

"*No—tres.*"

Then her hands were full of sugary things, dripping, and juice and sweet water ran down her chin.

WHEN SHE GOT HOME and Manuel let her in, nothing seemed to have changed. Rosalind sat upstairs on the terra-cotta porch, staring at the darkening sky.

"There you are," she said. Her face was wet as she pulled Alice close. "Have you eaten?"

Alice nodded. She always ate in the kitchen now with Maria, anyway. They watched the soap operas, and Maria's earrings dangled from the long holes in her ears as she shook her head sadly at the dramas.

"Brush teeth, then," said Rosalind. "And bed."

In the bathroom, Alice held the bubbly water in her mouth and swished it slowly back and forth, her cheeks bloated in the mirror. There were different passages in the throat, some that went down and others that went up; this she knew from doing drawings, like the drawings of the fish. And think of all those worms in the water, like tiny snakes or eggs. Funny that you couldn't feel or taste them, and how many were in one mouthful? Thousands, millions, swimming and darting, beautiful under the lens of a microscope, as everything always was. A tiny foreign world, green and yellow and living.

She swished the warm water back and forth in her mouth. She held it a moment longer, then maneuvered it a little farther back, and gargled. She returned it to her mouth. It was warm. She tilted her head from side to side and felt the water gently sloshing against the insides of her cheeks. Then she held her head straight and slowly swallowed. She stood there, looking at her pale face in the mirror, and opened her empty mouth wide. She filled a glass with water and drank it. Then another glass, and another, drinking and drinking until her body was all water, the water joggled inside her like a sea, full of tiny eels and water snakes and hunting, hunted, fish.

LATE THAT NIGHT, very late, Alice woke to the sound of a tinkling. The Miami glass beads that hung over her mirror jingled lightly against the glass. Her glass flower, too, tapped upon the mirror, tapped again and again. Her bed rocked. She sat up in the dark, listened to the tinkling beads, felt the shaking, then lay back down again.

So.

She shut her eyes and stretched out her arms, to float as the bed lulled and rocked, waiting. Beneath the bed, beneath the house and the city, far beneath in the dark, she was sure Pichincha and Cotopaxi and Chimborazo were stretching, shifting their vast muscles, their blood all liquid fire.

BUT THE NEXT MORNING everything seemed the same: just a little tremor, it hadn't done a thing. A few cracks ran through sidewalks, but they weren't even wide enough to stick a finger in. Most people had slept right through it.

Alice's stomach, though, had turned to quicksand. She lay and sweated, the room shivering away.

"*¿El agua?*" Rosalind asked Maria as they bent over the bed.

Maria looked at Alice's eyes.

It seemed then that she was always twisted in wet sheets, a child's sheets, sodden and salty. Sometimes Rosalind's face hovered near, her voice ringing and echoing like bells, but otherwise Alice kept falling through doors, falling into a white sky. But children did slip into other worlds through closets or glass; she knew this from books. There were other worlds where you could live in the roots and branches of trees, where you could breathe underwater. She saw these worlds and kept trying to let herself fall away, kept trying to wriggle free of that hand gripping her ankle and just be dropped into the sea, as all the while hands pulled back her sheets, peeled off wet pajamas, slid thermometers into her mouth.

At night she saw flashes of light made by the opening door, yellow bars lingering in the darkness. She never heard the voices anymore, but always there was a shuffling and thudding, as the house kept shedding them, shedding its contents.

But maybe they would all just go, and leave her, and forget?

Leave her in the sheets, or the long silky grass; leave her in the deep, soft sand.

*A*LICE WAS SICK for two and a half weeks, and when she was well, it was time.

The man who'd replaced Mr. Mueller, Bill Henz, drove them to the airport. Hal had sold the El Dorado to his replacement, so Mr. Henz drove them in his own car. Through the dirty streets, past the broad white buildings with roofs like wings, past the legless old men in wagons. Past the shops selling German clothes, and the cows, and the begging children with blackened hands. At the airport the crowd waited before the glass doors.

"Just go," whispered Rosalind.

They stood on lines; they boarded the Braniff; they buckled themselves into their seats.

When the plane took off, Alice pressed her forehead to the glass. She held her breath so as not to steam it and made an effort not to blink. The plane taxied, lifted, slowly climbed, and headed back over the city. The little terra-cotta and white roofs blurred; the green drained from pastures. Halfway up Pichincha, fields were burning, smoke drifting into blue.

PART II

I

Violet burst from the stifling house out to the veranda, stood a moment blinded by the morning sun, then went down the steps to the paddock, where Alf and the men were clearing. Such an old settler activity, clearing, when here it was, 1929. The hilly land was dry, the grass silvery and dotted with stumps of felled mallee. Along the edges of the paddock, beyond the stone house and sheds with corrugated-iron roofs, stood blackboys—spiky leaves with shafts rising from the center like ten-foot spears—and behind them were banksias and tall, twisted gums. Then everything dropped down to the sea, which stretched away blue to Kangaroo Island and the Great Australian Bight and beyond, to the bottommost edge of the world.

Alf and his brothers were driving shovels into the soil and every so often wrenching up a rock or a stump with its root, heaving them into piles. The plan was to fell the mallee, grub up the roots, treat the soil, make pastoral land. This was what Alf had said after his father died, when the land was divided among the brothers: given the terrain, it would have to be sheep. Once the roots were out, then the sheep would come and live a sweet life, and Violet and Alf would be off. Along the way they'd build their own house, away from the one the whole family now shared; it would be made in part from the mallee roots. They'd burn the roots in a kiln, together with the rocks of lime that lay all over the paddock, and from this they'd make a mixture to form blocks. So clever: but *that* Alf certainly was.

Violet watched with a hand shielding her eyes against the glare as Alf's brother, Harry, stood up from shoveling with a hand to his back and squinted into the trees. Then he gathered himself, bent, and heaved up a knotted root larger than his head. The roots were heavy, dense as rock, and reddish like petrified flesh. Violet could see that a wheelbarrow near the house was full of roots and rubble from the garden; they'd set up the lime kiln at the bottom of the hill, and it was really no trouble to wheel it down. She ran over the parched grass to the wheelbarrow, ignoring Harry's shouts for her to just *leave* it. Vi was like a bird with her pale blue dress and skinny arms and legs, even her head was thin, but for her size she was strong, burning with energy, her close-set eyes and bony hands quick, all of her darting in heat that would kill anyone weaker. But now Alf saw her from his end of the paddock, too, and began waving like a scarecrow, his voice thin in the air.

"No!" he shouted. "Vi!" As he always did when she came out to help; and as always, she ignored him.

"Back in with you!" he cried, coming nearer. Dust puffed around his feet, his baggy pants billowing. Inside them, she knew, his body was slim and smooth as a candle, and his dark hair stood up from the top of his head like a brush. His face was long, bookish beneath the hat, but his neck and hands were red and lined, and he was not meant for this life, having been (like herself) trained as a teacher. "I know you are a city lass," he had said only a year before. It was on one of the famous tennis weekends at her parents' house outside Adelaide, when they'd broken off from the others and strolled down the dry riverbed. "But all the same, Violet," he'd said, "I wonder if you could possibly consider a life of great ard—"

"Ardor!" she'd jumped in, blushing and fanning. Of course she'd known what he was about to say but wanted to make him blush, too, and stave off the event a few seconds.

"Well yes indeed certainly *ardor,* as you know! But it was *arduousness* I meant to say." Alf's brow grew grave again. "In a life spent with the likes of myself?"

Yes, Vi Clarence certainly would. The proposal had been prayed for and was salvation when it came, for it freed her from the cross of teaching, the training for which she had just completed and the prospect of which rose before her like a wall. But to make a home, a house, out in the bush—it felt like a doll's game, and sooner or later they'd move back to Adelaide, to shops and paved streets and ships with their sad horns, black Singer motorcars, moving pictures. But in the meantime, Vi Clarence was game, on for anything. Never fear! as they said.

Alf was waving his arms at her from across the paddock. "We need no help of yours here! Vi! Plenty to do inside!"

But she just turned her head and began steering the wheelbarrow down the hill and would *not* go back in—back to the domestic sphere, as they called it, making of it something grand. "Yours shall be the domestic sphere, my love," he had said, and she'd nodded, their hands clasped together at the table, the candle burning between them. Yet right now she'd been stifled to madness inside. Already she'd tidied the bedrooms and made the beds (working around Alf's mother, the ripe smell of her hair still clinging to Vi's arms), removed the ashes from the stove and sprinkled them into the long-drop lav in the outhouse, cut up hundreds of little squares of newspaper and set them in the box beside it, swept the carpets in the parlor, and mopped all the floors. If it were Monday, not Friday, she would do the washing, too, stirring the white pillow slips in the copper, lifting them into the cold water to rinse, turning them through the wringer, then washing the colors in the soapy water left behind. But it was not Monday, and to use water for that now would be a criminal waste. Yet she had such energy it seemed she'd burn to smithereens if she did not keep moving.

Violet maneuvered the wheelbarrow down the bumpy hill to the kiln. But now she realized that rolling the heavy wheelbarrow downhill was one thing, but lifting the handles enough to tip the roots was another. Alf and Harry and the others were leaning on their shovels, watching from the hill, as she struggled. She couldn't lift it with both hands, so she tried getting her shoulder under the handle and pushing up, but the thing wouldn't budge.

"Silly!" crowed Alf, to general mirth.

She cast them a look but then just abandoned the bloody wheelbarrow and ran laughing up the slope. Harry stalked down the hill to finish the job.

Vi wandered then in the bright sun, the dry grass brushing her ankles, and rubbed the shells in her pocket. This portion of paddock had already been cleared of mallee, the men moving farther off to where the grass was still stubbed with stumps. At the edges of the field, the bush grew wild again, giving way to blackboy and twisted gums. She kicked through the grass—until her foot struck a stump. A small one the men had missed.

The mallee roots were in truth beyond her, tough hard knots that were heavier than you'd think and clung tight to the soil, but this one was small. She would set herself against it, she decided; it would be her part in building the house. Dig and pry and scratch like a wild woman, and with luck she'd pull the thing out and be spent at last and then wilt like a lady on the veranda, fan herself and sip hot tea.

Violet got a spade from the shed, and came back and crouched in her forget-me-not dress, out in the glare and brittle grass. Here it looked like the hair of a towheaded child, although farther north it could be black, and even farther north, red dust.

She gripped a sheaf of grass, pulled it taut, and hacked it free. Then with her spade she started stabbing a ring around the stump, a dry moat in the soil. It was surprisingly hard.

"But I shall master you, no fear," she whispered. "Just watch. Just watch—Eleanor, or maybe Mildred. Or perhaps neither of those, but Humphrey."

It was terrifically hot. After hacking for a time she held her arms out at her sides and let the breeze blow through the dress. It was a breeze that seemed to blow up from the sea and then circle and blow out again, and it always seemed loud, full of voice and volume—as if just over your head urgent currents were rushing, pushing and pulling you back out to sea. Yesterday evening she had followed the path that wound down the cliff to the shore, and stood by the huge rocks, looking out. The rocks were black and razor sharp, jutting from the sand in long arcs like the spines of buried beasts. Some boulders were draped, by means of a geological event she could not fathom, with a thin pocked rock that looked exactly like tripe. Between the boulders, in pools, lay tiny blue top shells, and she had scooped up a handful and stood gazing south, where there was no more land to be reached, the bottom edge of the world. And surely the sea poured over that edge, a waterfall into space.

When she looked, the men had disappeared up the rise, dissolved in the morning glare. All she could see was the paddock, the house and outhouse, the splitting gums and their shabby branches; all she could hear was the breeze. She sat for a moment, listening. Then lifted her hand and touched it gently, like dipping a finger in water.

But back to the root. Her moat was deep, surely as deep as this root could have gone, and now she'd dig in to expose it. It wasn't very thoughtful work; what on earth did the men think about as they did it day after day? You hardly even had to look at what you did. You could just look around. The hilly paddock stretched out, and already, if you squinted to blur away the blackboy and gums, you could imagine the pale smudges of sheep here and there, how well this land would do for grazing once everything was improved.

"Nearly noon," she said aloud. She looked down at her dusty shoes, at her dress, which still showed nothing. "Nearly noon, Henrietta," she tried. "Or Herbert. *Herbert.*" She said the name again, but shook her head. It belonged to her father, and that's where it had better stay.

Chops, mashed spuds, beans from the garden: time to put the dinner on. The chops were thin and needed just a quick grilling, and the potatoes had been boiling for ages; they'd have mashed themselves by now.

2

An hour later, as the men trooped back out after dinner, Violet watched anxiously from where she stood washing up. Harry walked near her small clearing in the grass, noticed her spade lying there, and paused.

"No!" she cried. She struck the fly screen with a wooden spoon. "That one's mine! Hands off!"

He glanced back at her, shrugged, and went on.

She finished washing up and ran out with her hat. Around the stump her moat was deep, and the soil at the bottom felt almost cool to her fingers. She could already see the swelling knob of the root, which seemed more like a huge gourd than a root, well stuck in. When she hit it with the side of her spade, the blow rang up her arm.

All the same she would *have* this root. She would claim victory over this root!

From across the field, through the shimmering haze, Alf's small figure was waving again, his voice shrill in the air.

"I mean it, Vi! Truly! *Not* the work for you! Not now, for heaven's sake!"

She stood up so fast stars danced around her head, but she waved back at him vigorously. "Hoo hoo hoo!" she shouted, to annoy him.

For a few minutes the two of them stood there, two tiny figures in the landscape, waving. All around, the blanched land and peeling gum trees were motionless beneath the simmering sun, the sky enormous and vacant. After a time they both grew tired and fell still.

"Bossy," Violet muttered, dropping her arm. She would do as she pleased. Although Alf was a lovely man, gorgeous sense of humor. His hair had stood straight up from his head that day in the riverbed, such a thick soft brush rising from his yellow forehead that she suddenly had to plunge her hands into it. He was shocked (as was she), standing there with her hands submerged in his thicket, his hazel eyes beneath it unblinking, the red line of his spectacles still on his nose.

It had taken him months to ask. After all the weekends of tennis, all the picnics and organized outings, finally, at the end of a scorcher, they'd been wandering at dusk along the riverbed, reaching out now and then to tear away a hair of root poking from the soft red banks at either side. They got to a place where they had to duck because the roots crept over and formed a net above them; they had to clasp hands to keep balance as they lurched forward. By then it was nearly dark, and even after they'd passed under the netted roots, their hands were still clasped, and they stopped. Vi leaned against the loose bank, heart shivering inside her thin skin and thin dress. She remembered exactly the look of his shoes when he asked. "Would you consider . . . ?" But at that moment she was struck with the thought that a marriage proposal in a dried riverbed was *wrong*: it might have some ramification. She hurried to stopper his mouth, to press her damp hand against his lips. But like the warm air that blew along the riverbed as if it remembered the way, the question flew out, and there it was, before her. So—what else?—she laughed. Erupted. Knowing her thin cheeks were blotched with thrill and panic, that her crooked teeth and eyes were not lovely, she pressed her fingers into that thicket of hair and then seized his skeletal cheeks in both hands and kissed him with a lustiness that stopped such mystical fears as only a moment before had beset her, fears about improbable things.

Never fear!

Vi smacked her root with the side of the spade, and now that she could see it clearly she found it was the size of a bull's head. As she scraped around it, loosening the soil and then scooping it up so that little piles grew around her in the grass, out of the blue there came to her an old story about someone who built a marriage bed from the roots of a giant tree.

"Shall I tell you?" she said, looking down at her dress. She felt foolish and glanced around, but there was no one to hear her. So she cleared her throat and began, in a voice that even to her sounded made up.

"Once," she said, "there was a man who built a bed from the root of a tree."

Yet already she had to stop, resting her spade in the soil. "Or was it a whole house? But that was the Lost Boys. Flown away from wherever they got into trouble, run away to Never-Never Land. And there they hid in the roots of a tree, waiting for Wendy to sew their shadows back to their feet, so at least they'd know where they were, with respect to the sun and the earth."

Violet wiped her nose with the back of a dirty hand. She'd gotten things pretty wrong with that story. But wasn't it funny how it came down to sewing, so as not to be lost?

The Domestic Sphere! Although with respect to the sun and shadows matters were tricky: this she knew from her geographical studies. For here the sun moved across the sky in the north, not in the south as it did elsewhere, and this (she'd read) was a distressing alteration to those who had just arrived from England and Ireland, generations before. They had trouble accepting it, the sun in the north, and forgetting that the sun was not where it always had been, they mistook north for south and therefore west for east, and the world became even more upside down than they had realized it would be.

She squinted up at the bright sky, back down at her own squat shadow. She had never given the sun much thought.

If only, though, it weren't so *hot*. She adjusted the hat to better cover her neck, but that left a triangle of freckled chest bare.

In truth she was not enjoying this task and was sorry she'd begun. But she had already failed in front of them all with the wheelbarrow, and she still burned with such energy that she could not be in the house. She readjusted the hat.

"You shall wear a hat like this, Rosalind," she announced to her stomach. She tried the name again: *Rosalind*. That might be the one. "Or George. In case you turn out to be George." In honor of her forebear, as her father, Herbert, liked to call him. George Clarence, the one who'd first made the trip out.

When Alf finally asked, none of them had believed she could manage it. Marry! It didn't look likely, her sisters had said, that trio of big milky women. Whereas Vi was a twig, skirts yanked up to her skinny shins—although what her sisters didn't know was that she was not as daft as she looked. There were men who *liked* a sporting girl. A sporting lass, as they said: she camped in dry riverbeds and even the smelly dugouts of fishermen down at Willunga beach, scooping out a place to curl up in the sand and covering herself with an old Oriental; she rowed in the Torrens, and twirled her tennis racket, and swung her hockey stick on the dusty fields, her heels digging into the ground and leaving a trail of red cuts in the grass. Her sisters had pinched her thin, burned arms like witches.

But here she was, with Alf and a paddock and a root house coming, and now—Rosalind or Eleanor or George.

She paused in her digging, looked down at the thin cotton dress, and for a sudden moment, pictured her stomach and then right through her own skin, to the little thing that nestled inside her. A curve of tiny vertebrae and a small soft skull, like a newt, curled up in there in the dark.

She felt a little sick. Maybe this really was foolish. Maybe she should make herself sit in the house, like a lady in her condition. She put down her spade and dropped back on her haunches, inelegant but she didn't care. Her thin bare legs stuck out before her in the sun in the grass, and she smoothed her dress over her knees. Funny that this was the same old body she'd had as a girl in dugouts and branches, the same one her father had carried along the stream, the same bony calves and scabbed knees. She licked a finger and rubbed a knee, creased like the skin of a turtle. Or tortoise?

Of course she and Alf had both been trained as teachers; that was how they'd met. In her family there was no escaping it: both her father and her mother's father had taught. "You must be a teacher!" a voice had thundered to Herbert one night. "A mighty voice from the darkness," he reported, "and there I was, astonished and shaking, but this great voice summoned me, so what could I do?" He had risen trembling like someone in Dickens and obeyed the calling the very next day. She herself, when the time came, had been trained to teach home sciences. There was still a great need for young girls to learn sewing and cooking and laundering, just as there was a terrible need for boys to learn the agricultural arts. This is what her father said, this is what they said in school, and this she believed absolutely. The evidence had lain right outside the window. That great dry land, just one river to be counted on at all, the rest a network of red ditches all summer. It was fragile, they were told, the slight hold they had on their lives. They must never forget that they were still new in the land, scarcely a hundred years here, and that only scanty steps toward civilization had been made. So, dutifully, she had studied domestic arts and a smattering of the higher arts, too, English and even psychology and hygiene. She knew . . . oh, various things.

Violet sat up and took off her hat, smoothed her sweaty hair behind her ears, and set the hot hat right again. She knelt, straightened her dress, and picked up the spade. It was idiotic that she did this; one of the men could have done it fast with a shovel. Why hadn't she thought of a shovel? She got up and went to the shed.

It was dead dark in there, so she stood a moment, adjusting, enjoying the dizziness and the cool. In the bar of light made by the open door, a sketch of the house-to-be was tacked to the wall. A simple rectangular house made from those blocks of lime and burnt mallee. It would have a long, sloping tin roof that flattened out at the bottom to cover the veranda, and that is where they would sit, in cane chairs a step above the garden. A return veranda, with a sleep-out toward the back, the garden going clear around the house. Beans, peas, cabbages, cauliflowers, lettuces, cucumbers, and so on in one part, flowers in the front. Hollyhocks, gladiolus. Over near the gum trees, where the Coolgardie Safe stood full of milk and butter, they'd have a grove of lemon and mandarin trees.

And the dry sandy soil of the paddocks would be transformed; a wonder what could be done these days. Superphosphates, the agricultural people called the chemicals that could make this dead soil fertile. Some bags already leaned against the shed wall; they'd come, said their label, from the island of Nauru. Funny, something so exotic just to help her soil.

The men had taken all the shovels and crowbars. But it was to be *her* house, so she'd just have to keep at it with the spade. Because if only by virtue of having grubbed up one root, she could say she had helped build it.

"What do you think of that," she said, as she went back out to the blinding light and her root. "And you know"—she bowed her head, spoke softly—"I was never worried about any of it, the marrying, all the rest. Never fear!"

Never fear. She felt, when she said it, that she shook her fist to the sky. Of course it was something they all said, a silly phrase that meant nothing. But when she said it she *meant* it, tossing her head with the fine hair as wavy as she could make it with Curly Pet, her crooked eyes bright with determination. What good was fear? She did not have it in her. What she was set on doing was *living*.

"Go everywhere!" she cried, tossing soil onto a pile.

They all said they wanted to travel. But Violet meant it, a little ball of fire danced in her ribs, a tiny trapped sun that might fly from her throat. As a girl, she would put on her good hat and go with her sisters down to Port Adelaide to eat ices and watch the ships steam off. Just the smell of the sea and the sight of people waving on deck and the mournful, drunkening sound of the horn made tears fill her eyes, and that fire of longing blazed again and almost immolated her on the spot. Then slowly the ship would go: down the gulf, across the Bight, into the Indian Ocean, a great ship steaming to Britain. In the emptiness afterward Violet ate her ice tragically, tongue to the cold strawberry, quenching that fire.

"One day," she said to her sisters. "No fear! Just watch me. I shall go."

"Oh but *where,* Violet," they said, yawning. "Wherever shall you go."

"Everywhere! All over! Home."

When the word came out it surprised her, for she stood not twenty miles from where she'd spent every day of her life. Home! The word meant nothing. "Do stop calling Britain *home,* Ruth," Herbert had so often said to her mother, when she stood outside the bluestone house gazing bitterly at the fallen jacaranda pods and strips of gum bark littering her roses and jonquils and love-in-a-mist. Ruth hated those gums and the sticky drops they oozed, hated the landscape altogether, and held herself close, even though she'd been born right in Adelaide. "You are a native Australian, plain and simple," Herbert would say. "It's nonsense, this 'home' business, a colonial affectation." For by "home" Ruth meant England, pure England, not even Ireland, although in truth that was where her own family was from.

And lo and behold Violet had said the same thing. She'd never even thought about it until the word flew from her mouth at the port. She laughed it off, while her sisters looked on, disdainful. Yet something tugged as the girls journeyed back into hot land, and she could not help but feel she was traveling the wrong way.

Violet looked up now, squinting out over the shimmering field. The sky was a hot chalky blue beyond the trees' white branches; a butcher-bird suddenly fluted. In the haze at the edge of the paddock, the blackboys looked like real black boys might once have, crouching in the bush with their spears up for threat. A drop of sweat rolled down her nose and she let it dangle at the tip, swaying her head gently to see how long it would hold, until at last it fell into the soil. The back of her neck was baking.

"But now I remember," she said aloud. "In fact it *was* a bed, not a whole house, that fellow built from the roots of a tree. A tree that was still rooted."

Although which story this belonged to still escaped her. But a bed made in a rooted tree—a sign of fidelity for sure.

Already Violet had thought more about trees today than she had in her entire life. They were just there, with their bark and flossy blossoms, and with luck they gave some shade; the sheep would be happy to find them. The Coolgardie Safe stood beneath the tree nearest the house—and she suddenly realized it needed water.

At any rate, *she* did. The sweat had been sliding down her freckled arms and slipping between her breasts, and she could not have a drop left in her. She and her skin did not belong in this place!

"When I was a baby," she began again in her made-up voice, as she brushed the dirt from her hands and rose, "I had such a delicate skin that the slightest exposure made me blister and peel. So Father would take me in his arms at dusk and carry me along a creek, even when the creek was dry, because the breeze ran there anyway."

Suddenly she was struck by the coincidence. Her father and those evenings along the creek, and camping in dry riverbeds as a girl, and then, years later, Alf and the famous proposal. As if a dry river had always run alongside her. Not to mention the pull of that sea breeze, tugging and urging you away . . .

Stiff, she blundered in the brightness toward the well by the shed. They had several bores on the property, but this one gave the sweetest water. She filled a bucket and carried it over to the Coolgardie, splashing wet streaks on her dusty shins. She refilled the pan on top and none too soon, for the hessian cloth that was draped from the pan and over the chest to cool it when the breeze blew through, evaporating, was nearly dry, and that would have been a fine waste of milk. Back at the tap she drank, splashed the back of her neck, and let water trickle down her front.

"We are being bloody stupid," she said.

Suddenly the dogs were barking, and dust hovered above the road from a car driving up to the house: the hawker. She patted her cheeks, ran into the house, and wondered what he'd have today.

"Good day, Mrs. Edwards!"

She held the veranda door to him wide and then hurried to the kitchen for a glass of water while he arranged his wares.

3

LATER, WHEN THE hawker had gone, Violet sat on in the parlor, feeling dull. A worn round rug lay on the floor, the clock upon the mantelpiece ticked, Alf's mother's people stared balefully out at her from framed photographs on the wall, and down the hall the old woman herself snored with a sound like a crow. Violet sat slumped in a curlicue chair and wondered what had come over her.

It must have been all the *things*. All those little objects the hawker had brought for her to look at and imagine having, curtains and cosmetics and kitchen gadgets. Between the bag of magic stuff from Nauru and the uncustomary thoughts she'd been thinking as she dug and now this, this bit of French cloth she'd just bought, she had the inflamed, confused sense of having traveled.

And it was only half past three! They'd want their tea at six, but everything was ready, just as the house was perfectly tidy, and down the hall Alf's mother still slept, so there was nothing to be done.

The clock ticked more loudly. For a moment she felt a scream swell in her throat. She stood abruptly, put on her hat, and went back out to the root.

All the hawker's packets and bundles . . . but she was glad he came, given they were halfway in the bush. That forebear, George Clarence, whoever he was, the first of the line to have come out, must have arrived when Adelaide didn't even exist, when everything still had to be brought and built. What did you do? Just land here, look around, scrape something up out of dirt? Why did he even come? All that was left of him was a ripped old photograph: a large man with a shattered face standing by a tree. It might have been a she-oak, part of the picture seemed to be swaying, blurred. He stood among its boughs as if for protection, and there was an idea that he had been deaf. His big trunk was packed into a tight, faded coat, and he had close-set eyes, uncomfortable large hands. His arms were clenched at his sides, one tightly gripped by a birdlike hand. A woman, his wife? But the rest of her had been torn away, leaving a furred, dirty edge of paper. Even her name on the back was torn off, there were just a few words, mostly smudged. Violet's father had studied this document again and again, as if one day the words would come whole. All it said for sure was *George Clarence,* then the tear and a smudge that looked like *Salt* or *Saint* something, then *Scotl;* even the rest of that word was gone. That was all. So, he'd been Scottish, but one could only guess why he'd come. With all the schoolteachers who'd followed in his line, though, the math had been done again and again, and he couldn't have come before 1836, as Adelaide was first being scratched from the bush—when they were still building the port, laying the streets, bringing over Britain bit by bit.

In her own father's time, when he was a lad, as he said, the shopkeeper in town was a curious sort, a hybrid, her father said, between Old World and Australia. He had a telescope, in addition to all the goods the town needed, and he himself had ground the lens—as if, said Herbert, this ability were vestigial of the greater nearness to Europe still extant in those early days. This telescope the shopkeeper had mounted upon a platform in his garden (itself a testament to those vestiges, for it was full of exotic Dutch bulbs he'd shipped in), and, at the appropriate time of the month, he would invite neighbors and any visitors of interest to come and view the moon. In his dark garden with its voluptuous blossoms, the unaccustomed, earthbound viewers would climb up to the platform, take a glimpse, and then draw away, disoriented. The surface of the moon—reported Herbert as a boy to his fellows, and then, years later, to Violet—the surface of the moon was exactly like tripe.

"Tripe again!" she said, flinging down her spade. She touched the shells in her pocket and, shutting her eyes to the afternoon glare, saw again the pocked stone that draped the other rocks in the cove.

"Tripe, of all things," she whispered. She had a brief, curious sense of things spinning, of her own rocky cove being part of the moon, of this place where she lived being suddenly far removed from another place, where someone was standing, at the other end of a telescope, looking at Violet herself.

She picked up her spade and continued poking. It was maddening the way the thing clung. She could knock it with all her might and it would not budge.

That shopkeeper had other interests, too, some of which (said her father) veered near the occult, but in those days, abstruse arts were popular. He kept in close touch with England and Europe—what with all the back and forth of his wares—

and one fascination he developed was mesmerics. Thus he looked far afield, this unusual shopkeeper, as far as the moon and the farthest reaches of space, but also deep into the human soul. And once he had fixed his customers with a bright mariner's eye and told of the wonders he'd seen, they too were possessed. A certain young woman in town soon distinguished herself as particularly susceptible to mesmeric trances. When she was in her trance, you could present her with any object, said Herbert, its identity known only to yourself, and she, blindfolded and merely touching it, would concentrate, tremble like a chord, and finally pronounce in a voice from another world the original home of the thing.

One evening she was given a small piece of pumice that had been blown from Mount Vesuvius. Turning it around between her fingers, she felt the light porous stone, all its airy dimples and holes. After a spell of concentration, she finally began to speak, and it was like the Sibyl herself from the Underworld. She drew an astonishing portrait: of the deepest innards of that famous volcano. It was truly as if, said Herbert—his face still as full of wonder as it surely had been that evening fifty years earlier—as if she were *inside Vesuvius herself.* "Inside the very volcano," he whispered.

Violet poked at her root. Then she looked tentatively around the root; she looked into the earth. It was dense, heavy, and lightless.

She felt as if she kept flying free of her tether, or as if the center of things kept shifting and she had to work to keep herself fixed.

"Like sewing on the shadow," she said.

She paused a moment. Things were getting unclear.

"Back to the Lost Boys' feet, I mean." She shook her head and touched her stomach and looked down at her forget-me-not dress.

"Eleanor, Rosalind," she said then, with some effort. "No. I think Rosalind. Unless you really *are* George."

That long-lost forebear, far before her own time. Finally working her spade under the mallee root now, she thought of the phrase *my own time*. She stopped working a moment, irked.

Out of the blue she understood: there was a thin strip of time that was hers, and all the vast rest of it was not.

She blinked, wiped her cheek. "Aren't you having radical thoughts," she whispered into the empty air. But then she was convulsed in giggles—for what else to have but radical thoughts when grubbing up a *root*? *Radix, radicis:* she'd learnt enough Latin from her dad to know *that*.

And so her mind went to radishes and cucumbers, and whether there would be rain soon for the garden, and whether the dogs would keep the bloody rabbits away . . .

More energetically, then, encouraged, Violet worked the spade under the root, wedging and prying—but with no response. She slumped back and stared at the damnable thing. Her hands hurt, as did her knees.

But think of those forebears and what they'd surely endured! Her father spoke of them as Lares and Penates. But it was frustrating how unclear things got only four generations back, nothing known but *Scotl*, as if the first of the line had just stepped from the soil one day. That baffled Great-great-grandfather George Clarence, that oversized Scot, maybe deaf. Had he come looking for luck? Or was he a convict and made his way later to South Australia? And if so, what was his crime?

"When thou tillest the earth, it shall not henceforth yield unto thee her strength—a fugitive and a vagabond shalt thou be on the earth!" she sang out.

She dug and scraped and pressed the heels of both hands

against the back of the spade to try to get farther under the bloody obstinate root. She wondered if he was truly deaf. Maybe he just looked deaf, in the picture. But how could you *look* deaf? Maybe a little off-kilter. The way he stood shrinking into the boughs of that she-oak, he seemed so stricken, so far from home. At least he had that birdlike hand on him, that woman there, a tether.

"Ulysses!" Vi cried suddenly, throwing her spade into the grass. "Ulysses. Fancy remembering, out of the blue. He's the one who built the bed from a rooted tree. And then set off to war and got a god angry, and was sent on years of wandering."

She hummed, high pitched, and shut her eyes. They had been so trusting, George Clarence and all those others who had come long ago. Putting their trust in God as they stepped onto wooden vessels that would bear them, they prayed, over the Atlantic, around the Horn, across the Indian Ocean.

She looked up, put a hand on her breast, sat straight, and began to intone to the bright field:

> *"Here I raise mine Ebenezer;*
> *hither by Thy help I'm come;*
> *and I hope, by Thy good pleasure,*
> *safely to arrive at home."*

Such a hard shining thing that faith must have been! Those men must truly have *believed* as they faced the treacherous sea, and then as they faced this land.

She herself had never given faith much thought. No more than she'd given trees or the sun. And as she began to do so now, she felt uneasy.

She decided to think about something else. What about all those travelers and explorers who preceded her forebears? The very first ones—like Captain Hook?

She dropped her head, realizing the mistake.

It was stinking hot, the sweat stinging and blurring her eyes, and things were becoming confused. For she'd meant Captain *Cook,* not Hook, not Peter Pan's Captain Hook. Whose hand had been bitten off by a croc as he chased the Lost Boys in Never-Never Land.

But Never-Never—was it *the* Never-Never? Here? Up north? Was that story all about *here,* then? That story about Wendy and the Lost Boys, who'd run away from somewhere? What with the natives and so on, Tiger Lily about to be drowned?

Violet shook her head and stood up, but one foot was pins and needles, so she hopped over the grass to where she'd thrown her spade. Bloody, bloody foolish, what she was doing. She wanted a cup of tea, she wanted a nap, she was *spent,* and that was rare.

Imagine Cook and those explorers and colonists and the rest setting sail. Taking leave of family, gathering belongings, stepping onto a piece of wood and floating on the water. Nothing but water, nothing but sky—and at night, nothing but stars.

She felt seasick imagining this. Funny that you might better know where you were at night than by day. Keeping track of where you floated upon all those leagues of sea according to where the stars hung in the depths of blackness above. All they had were those lines drawn from their eyes to the stars, and from the stars back to London, so that they could plot themselves according to that fixed place, home.

Violet rubbed her eyes and looked around at the blowing

dry grass. Her hands stung; an arc of blisters had erupted on both red palms.

She stood abruptly, but, pins and needles again, her leg buckled beneath her and she lurched in a flurry of dust, and had to sit down again and slap at her leg until it came back to life.

She peered into the damnable hole. How few bones there must have been in the soil, back when those settlers arrived. An eerie soil empty of bones. And *deep*. She'd never much thought about it. But of course it was deep—as deep as the ocean. No, deeper. She could not take such depths in. She felt sick. It was hot. And bright! And her skin had not been made for this place! Already her thin arms were as scorched as Alf's.

But again she crouched and continued to dig. When a blister on her right hand broke open and bled she swapped the spade to her left. Sweat ran down her nose and hung at the tip, and she strained with her tongue to catch it. People wandered and wandered, and what did it mean, where on earth did they ever *belong*? They weren't plants, after all.

She felt lunatic. She put her hands to her burning cheeks.

What she meant was, if people weren't plants and didn't grow from the ground, how could they ever *belong* anywhere? What was home?

She sat for a moment on her haunches, unhappy. And how strange it was, how very strange, the way people existed as surely as she did and then disappeared in the earth altogether.

She plunged the spade in again.

Yes, well, with every strike against this root she was jolly well coming closer to home, wasn't she? Closer to building their bloody house!

It was stinking, stinking, stinking hot! As if that restless fire inside her that had started this idiot endeavor had burnt right through and now raged at her skin. Her dress clung to her back and between her slippery legs, and she tugged it free, reddening, although surely by now her skin was as red as it could be, roasting out here in this blazing sun.

Violet threw down her spade and stared at the root. It lay there like a buried thing, obstinate, as if it and the earth were in cahoots and the last thing they'd do was give way.

She was a filthy fool and she hated herself, for by now the men had grubbed up dozens of stumps and moved far off into the glare, and there was nothing to prove to anyone. But she could not leave it, and it would not budge, the bloody, bloody root! She stared at it; she scrambled to her feet far too quickly and kicked it despite the spinning stars. It was hard, harder than stone, a nasty tight coil of living spiteful rock, enough to break your bones upon.

Then she *would* break her bones upon it! She would! She threw herself facedown and gripped the spade with both hands and tore at the soil around the boulderlike root. Her knees and elbows dug in, as she pried at the thing from every side, plunging the spade furiously into the soil, the blisters on both hands now open and bleeding.

ALL AROUND THE PADDOCK the gum trees rustled, shedding a strip of bark to cool a trunk, easing an old branch looser. The breeze moved through the blackboy spears, and the seeds in the long stalks rattled. A pair of cockatoos tumbled from the sky and settled among the white branches; a galah in turn soared up.

And meanwhile Violet fought in the grass, sobbing, nose running, up to her elbows in soil where a root lay buried like a primordial skull. She got to her knees and hacked and stabbed; she struggled to her feet and squatted and pulled. She pressed her filthy shoes to either side of the thing, and bent and wrenched . . .

And finally the thing broke free. With the shock of it she staggered back, but there the root was, dangling before her face, a twist of soily dark hair in her fingers.

ALL OVER THE PADDOCK was a stillness, a calm: among the white trees, whose long leaves were full of oils that could burst into flame but then grow back easily from a blackened stump; among the banksias, which for several million years had not borne such a name; among the sulfur-crested cockatoos, the tiny lizards, the black snakes resting in the grass; among the magpies and butcher-birds that blinked and waited in the branches.

Violet held the heavy root before her with trembling hands. A dead thing, a live thing, a vengeful thing sticky with earth.

Suddenly a spasm went through her, and she laughed— a shriek that flew into the dry air and fell away into silence. She dropped the root to the ground.

ONCE, SIXTY YEARS EARLIER, a boy had gone lost in Victoria. A small boy, only seven. It happened in a gully during a picnic with his mother and friends. They wore silk Victorian clothes and sat upon Oriental rugs, with their parasols and teapots, among the ancient tree ferns and tangling vines that had made the gully famous as far away as London, where a painting of the place had once been shown.

Having had his sandwich and cup of sweet milky tea, the boy set off exploring. Perhaps he was drawn by the stream, which sometimes glowed when the antipodean sun fell upon it through the feathery tops of the tree ferns, and sometimes was black and cool in deep shadows, meandering between rocks that had lain beneath the sea millions of years earlier, when the continent had another shape and dwelled elsewhere. Perhaps the boy just could not resist the way one flat broad rock led to another, forming inhuman steps, so that sometimes he climbed up, sometimes he climbed down, and sometimes he had to squeeze between rocks that pressed close and high, a chasm. So off he went wandering, a little Scottish Australian boy with short pants and creamy skin, following the stream that wound through the ancient gully.

By the time it grew dark he was lost. He could not remember which way he'd come, and only wandered farther. Then he got even more confused and forgot which way he'd just been walking, so that he ran first one direction, then another, farther and farther away.

They searched for him that night and all the next day; they searched for several weeks. Finally, though, they had to give up. He was never found. But many years later, someone discovered in a hollow tree trunk a boy's neat little bones, curled up and hiding.

It was the end of the day now, the shadows from the eucalypts drifting across the waving grass. The breeze blew more strongly, smelling of sea, streaming over the paddock, over the cliff, and out again to the ocean. Just above Violet's head, currents of air tugged and pulled. A bank of low clouds lay upon the sea, darker than the water. In the trees along the edge of the paddock the butcher-birds were fluting.

Violet looked down at her shoes. She moved one in the caked earth. She wiped her hands on her dress and walked away from the hole, away from the root that lay beside it; over the grass, the familiar flaxen grass, warm and dry at her ankles, past the shed, toward the bit by the house that was almost green from where she tossed the dirty water, and up the stone steps to the veranda. She held a hand lightly to her stomach, warm through the thin cotton dress. From the paddock behind her came the voices of Alf and his brothers as they made their way home, looking forward to tea.

PART III

I

⁜

THE MEN WITH their axes and torches would soon be there;
they were already climbing the steep path up the bluff, and
Mr. Clarence's house stood between the bluff and the shore,
the last house on the island. The grass around it was streaming like water, the wind blowing as strong as the sea. On the
rocky beach, waves were smashing. The apple trees by the
house bent and moaned.

"There's no time," said Mr. Clarence, pulling George
from the window.

They stumbled down the dark hall, George huge and
mute, his crooked eyes panicked, his large chapped hands
grasping candles and pots; Mr. Clarence slight in a shabby
blue coat, his white hair flying around a face like a very old,
stricken child's. They snatched clothes from drawers, dishes
from cabinets, cutlery, a lamp. They threw everything into a
wooden chest, and George dragged it down the stone steps
and out to the bright green and wind.

From beyond the bluff smoke gusted into the sky, and George stopped on the grass, breathing hard, and stared up. The factor and his men had already turned the bend in the path and were halfway up the cliff. When they reached Mrs. Maidlin's, they'd set it on fire, and when they got down here, they'd smash up the house. Not just the house but the apple trees, too, they'd chop them down and tear up the garden, because everything was being cleared off the island.

It was 1822, and English *improvements* were under way. The land was worth nothing with these Scots on it, so they were being uprooted and shipped over the sea, the land cleared for betterment, for sheep. Already thousands of people had sailed to America. Mr. Clarence himself wasn't a Scot, but he'd settled among them, so he too was being removed, and as he and George were nearly father and son, there was no question of their parting. When the notice had been nailed to the door, Mr. Clarence just stared at it, then cleared his throat and tried to explain, and George felt that pounding in his head and began rocking on his heels. They only must leave, Mr. Clarence promised, no one would be harmed. He'd written to his brother in London for help, but the clearing had started a week early.

Last night old Mrs. Connell had wandered naked and weeping along the shore, for her house was gone, the men had burned it, together with her clothes. But she was so old and baffled she thought she'd misplaced it, that it was just a matter of remembering where. And the day before, beyond the bluff, Brian Donaldson would not leave his bed, so the men had hacked the place down around him. He lay out there still, shocked and chattering, his bed in the blowing meadow.

George swayed on the windy grass, looking down at all the familiar things so foreign in the sunlight. Mr. Clarence's straight chair and Bible: they seemed as shocked as Mr. Clarence was, the sun bright on the dark polished wood, wind ruffling the gold-edged pages. They looked like buried creatures exhumed.

Mr. Clarence appeared at the door. "George!" he cried. "I can't think what else—no—the letter—" He disappeared in the house, and George began to follow but then saw the men on the bluff, the flames of their torches, a glint of sun on an ax. The roaring began in his ears, and he couldn't help it, he ran.

George knew all about men with axes. They were one thing he knew, along with the trees in the orchard and the fact that the ground beneath him was packed with heads and hands and the slow soaking blood of fathers and mothers, and that now it was happening all over again.

He ran into the orchard and hummed as he patted at a dry trunk, at a smooth living knob like an elbow. These were the trees into which he'd run as a boy—run from where he couldn't remember, the idea of home was a black hole in his mind. But from what he'd run he knew, for he ran from it still. The bloody horrors that had leached into his skull and dwelled there ever since: the sound of that head cloven, the flames roaring up, the ax sinking into her neck, then the look in her eyes as she fell. He had run for days and nights and stumbled into this orchard. A strange place, for in this part of the world were only heather and moors. The trees stood around him like secretive company, much more peaceful than men. He grew calm there, and curled up in the roots and dried leaves. The next morning Mr. Clarence was staring down at him. He gave George an apple and crouched, waiting for him to speak, but already George's tongue was like his mother's head—not cut off, but dead in his mouth. Because if he let his tongue be dumb, be animal, he'd stay safe and apart from that world of men. Mr. Clarence lifted him gently and tried to bring him to the house, but George ran back into the trees. So Mr. Clarence let him stay. He brought him clothes, fed him, even gave him his name, but George stayed where he belonged. After a time it became clear that he was a born gardener, and he'd been there ever since.

Mr. Clarence was apart from men, as well. Although George didn't speak, over the months and years he listened as Mr. Clarence murmured, and looked on with his crooked, troubled eyes. The two misplaced figures worked side by side in the orchard, the older man small, tattered, and pink, George ever larger and more bearish. Mr. Clarence had fled to that island, too, but for him it was because of guillotines, despair, a feeling, he tried to explain, that his world was ending. That a new one gaped open, faithless and grim. His brother, he told George, made soap in London, and when the French wars broke out and there were embargoes he'd needed a fresh source of something that happened to be found in seaweed. So Mr. Clarence had taken the chance to flee, happy to give these poor Scots a living gathering the kelp that washed up on the shore. That was the official reason he'd come. Secretly, though, it was to be away from that world he had such trouble understanding, and instead to ponder God. For he believed only in God's Word, that God's voice hovered all around, and he really imagined that, with enough effort, one day he would hear it. He hoped, he said, to live just a little as God wished Man to dwell in His Creation. Simply, doing no one harm, revering what was offered, until at last he could shut his eyes and be Home. He laughed and flushed when he said this, because it seemed so clear yet so far-fetched. He was always listening for His voice, looking for signs of His wishes, gazing with wonder at the sea and sky He had made.

George tried but understood nothing of God, although what he felt for Mr. Clarence might come close. He heard no voice but Mr. Clarence's, and he understood only his own breath and the air it met outside him, his own blackened hands and the soil and trunks into which, as he worked, they sometimes dissolved.

The rustling leaves, the warm green smell, the wrinkled skin of the trunks—these trees seemed to him like life perpetual, as if they had always existed and would live on forever. They seemed to him more real, more fixed, than the world of men. And what George longed for, what deep in his dark mind he imagined was home, was a place that simply existed without men, a place before or after them. And he knew, because Mr. Clarence had told him, that there was still a New World that hadn't been touched. It rose from the sea like the green back of an animal, and its riotous birds could be heard even over the crashing waves, birds no one had seen, land no one had stepped on, and Dear God, Mr. Clarence had said, Dear God, please keep it safe from us. George saw it, in dreams. It didn't look quite like this world but warmer, more wild. He woke from the place drenched and longing.

Up on the bluff now the men surrounded the cottage. There was the sound of shouting, fists beating the door. Then the crack of a hatchet striking wood, and among the cries of the seagulls rose a woman's voice, high and thin. Black smoke lifted into the sky, and after a sucking pause, flames flared. So they were done already. Mrs. Maidlin was up there, a dark form standing on the edge of the bluff, the little children running around her. The men advanced down the bluff, sunlight glinting from their blades.

George hummed loudly, clutching at branches. They were the same men, they were always the same, who came with axes in his dreams. Blood pounded in his head, and he pressed his face into the leaves. He felt himself running, felt his bones crashing into that wild, green, more ancient world, but he couldn't, there was nowhere to go.

Boots crunched on gravel. There was a smell of sweat and damp smoke.

The factor strode across the yard and stopped at the desk and trunks on the grass.

Mr. Clarence appeared in the doorway. "You are too early," he said. "It was to be next week. It is not right, you may not—"

"Couldn't be helped," said the factor. He stepped forward.

"But where are we and all these people—"

"Get on," said the factor. "You know what we must do."

"It isn't just!" said Mr. Clarence. But the factor pushed past him into the house, Mr. Clarence after him.

George began to follow but the men came forward. His ears burned, and he stepped behind a tree trunk.

One of the men laughed. "He thinks we can't see him! A bloody giant like that. Off," he said, and shook his ax. "The orchard must go down."

But George just dissolved into the tree, into the rustling leaves, the green air, the bark cool against his forehead.

The man moved closer as the factor came back out. "What is he then—an idiot?"

"For God's sake, Mr. Clarence, call your man away!"

Mr. Clarence faltered into the light. "George," he began from the doorway.

But George was humming and lost and didn't move, and surely if he shut his eyes and let that shrillness fill his ears and pushed his head hard against the trunk, it would happen, these men would slide back into earth, slip down and be lost among the old muddy bones, never have arisen at all.

The factor signaled to begin.

"Please!" cried Mr. Clarence. He came down the steps as the men headed into the garden. "Wait—until he's gone and will not have to see."

The factor turned away. "Begin, Donald."

"Please!" cried Mr. Clarence.

But the ax flashed and struck the young trunk beside George with a crack. The tree shuddered and split, and leaves showered down, a raw green smell in the air.

"Look at him, the idiot's blubbering," said Donald, wiping his face.

"Carry on."

"It'll hit him this time—"

"Carry on!"

"Just move away now, will you?"

"George!"

"As you like."

Donald was drawing back to swing when Mr. Clarence reached him. "George," he said, "George, come away, it's all done."

GEORGE AND MR. CLARENCE rode by wagon to Oban, past men dismantling and burning cottages and uprooting meager crops. All the way Mr. Clarence stared. He looked as shocked and forsaken as the place, his watery eyes and white hair wild as if things were streaming by much too fast. This world of industry and advancement—Mr. Clarence had shut his eyes and run from it once, and now he must run all over again, and what troubled George was that he could not run fast enough. Now and then he roused himself and raised a hand for George to stop the horses, and he slipped down to give a few coins to a family leaving.

"Finished," he said then, as they rode on. "That is what I

feel." He sat silent for a time, and finally said, "But I *know* there is a Purpose." And he gazed up at heaven with his bright child's eyes, his old veined hands clenched together, his small hopeful mouth murmuring, praying, and what worried George now was that what Mr. Clarence believed in was not there, it had never been there, and why wasn't the *sky* enough?

They waited at Oban for several days, until Mr. Clarence had word from his brother and shut his eyes in relief. They would sail to Plymouth, he told George, and then to Saint Michael, a Portuguese island in the Atlantic. A blessing. They would move to a small citrus plantation that had been his uncle's but was now a ruin. So, he told George, trying to smile, they would start anew, in oranges.

"I hope you won't mind that it's so far." He patted George's big freckled hand.

But George hardly minded. The farther and more solitary the place the better. He hadn't belonged here, he didn't belong among men, he would always shamble away from them. He gripped the reins, and as the wagon took them to the harbor he could feel the earth and all the shattered bones and skulls packed within it jamming hard against the wheels.

IT WAS 1822. All over the globe civilization was advancing; things were being transformed, unearthed, transplanted. Scots were shipped to North America, British convicts to New South Wales; the natives there were cleared off to make room. Sir Joseph Banks had recently died, but his plant hunters toiled on in foreign lands, sending exotics home to Kew. Ship after ship sailed the globe, like arks, with men and women below deck and green plants above. Wattle and eucalypts from Australia, jacaranda from the Argentine, bougainvillea from Brazil. The living world was rearranged.

Just under ground, deeper changes were in store. In Sussex one afternoon, a Mrs. Mary Mantell spotted several teeth poking from some rubble. Several *enormous* teeth that were heavy and filled her hand; it was not clear to what creature they belonged. In cliffs and quarries all over the globe, embedded in sandstone and clay, kindred skulls, fractured jawbones, and curving spines lay waiting for the men who would soon be dubbed "scientists" to puzzle out what they meant.

Coal was being dug up, too, now more than ever. Coal that had once been living tree ferns, a fact the new geologists were beginning to fathom; the term "Carboniferous" had recently been coined. Coal was fed into the steam engines that had at last been perfected and now powered cotton mills and locomotives. Coal-run engines could even be fitted to ships, so that in the few decades since Captain Cook had found the last continent and carved Britain's claim to it upon a gum tree, exotic plants and Scots and sugar and cotton could be sped from one continent to another. The industrial revolution was under way.

Political revolution, as well. Liberty, equality, independence! First America had broken from England; then the French revolted against monarchy; Haiti rose up against France; and Spanish America fought for independence from Spain. Now revolution filled the air in Brazil.

This is where the Portuguese royal family had gone when Napoleon's armies drove them from home. Now the rest of the family had returned to Lisbon, but the eldest son, Pedro, having smelled revolution, decided to stay in his tropical colony. Soon he was emperor of independent Brazil.

Across the Atlantic, his younger brother Miguel cursed that he had not been the one to stay and that the empire had lost its best colony. Conflict between brothers looked likely.

2

*F*ROM OBAN GEORGE AND Mr. Clarence sailed with the writing desk, trunks, and chair down to Plymouth, where they waited to board a ship for the Portuguese Azores. The port was seething as they made their way through it, George sweaty and lumbering, Mr. Clarence slight and nervous beside him. Bales of cotton, sacks and crates of sugar and tea, barrels of tar and pitch were heaved from man to shouting man. On the decks, Scots bound for North America clasped bundles of clothing and stared at the world they were leaving; pale convicts in chains listed in the air before the long passage to the other side of the world. The air was sour with bodies, meat, raw goods, and fish, and loud with shouts and the creaking of ships.

Farther down the dock a crowd gathered, and George climbed on a barrel to see: a dark man in paint and chains and another with sticks piercing his skin, both naked, were being unloaded from a ship. Up on the deck, a merchant leaned into a crate and pulled out a gleaming vase. Another produced something like it and held it up to the sky. It took a moment to register the skull's eye sockets, the blue sky shining through.

"Aboriginal," the merchant called to a sailor.

George and Mr. Clarence hurried on. Among all the ships laden with people and goods was one with something different. On its decks stood glass cases, fogged and spattered with salt. A sailor opened one and pulled out a plant that he slung over his shoulder, carried to the dock, and set down. When he returned to the ship, George came near.

It was a palm tree, with a skinny, hairy trunk and plumage of bright green fans. George had never seen anything like it—it was nothing like his apple trees—but as he crouched beneath it, he felt a shock, as if he'd seen it before. Sunlight fell yellow through the shifting fronds, and the trunk was soft as fur to his hand. It seemed primeval, part animal, wild. As if it came from another world, a world he almost recognized.

Sailors carried down more plants and set them on the dock, and by the time Mr. Clarence reached him, he stood in a jungle. Spiked evergreens with whorling arms, hairy trunks topped with delicate feathers, plants with flopping, translucent leaves, all shivering in the English sun.

"Exotics," murmured Mr. Clarence. "Curious what they're finding, all those botanists sent out from Kew."

They stood on the creaking wooden dock, salt water slapping the posts, and looked at this misplaced menagerie. But Mr. Clarence didn't seem to see the same thing George saw. His eyes were lit, as if by a sign, a comforting reminder of God's hand upon Creation.

—————

THEIR SHIP WAS a schooner built for the citrus trade, with room for just three passengers. Along with George and Mr. Clarence traveled a Mr. Dunn, in lemons.

"Joining the trade?" he asked as they stood on deck and the ship made its slow way from the harbor. "Saint Michael?"

Mr. Clarence nodded. "Oranges." He smiled politely but looked away, hands clutching each other in the salty wind.

Mr. Dunn leaned forward. "An excellent business, Saint Michael's oranges. Eighty years ago the first few were shipped to England, and now—four hundred thousand crates each year to London alone, each with five hundred oranges. And seven thousand crates of lemons. Just do the arithmetic to ascertain the extent of the market—"

"Yes," said Mr. Clarence. "We do hope." He smiled again, then turned away and stared out to sea. Mr. Dunn opened a newspaper.

Those first days, the sky was dirty, the sea whipped with storms. The schooner rode waves like valleys and hills, and water slashed over the decks; at breakfast, eggs and cups wobbled across the table, and seawater splashed in, dousing the toast. Sea and air seemed to churn together, and Mr. Clarence crept to his cabin, leaving George to walk around and around the deck, water streaming down his shaggy head.

As Mr. Clarence lay shivering in his hammock, vomiting into an enamel bowl George had put on the floor, the ship rocked and plunged. Beneath them, the sea dropped in cold depths of water no one had ever seen, down to a barren shifting floor that was unimaginably old. And around them the world they'd fled kept advancing, Empire creeping across every continent, clearing what lay in its path.

When the storm was over, Mr. Clarence emerged and leaned unsteadily on his stick on deck. Here in the middle of the ocean the sky was like a new sky, merciless and brilliant, and the sea blinded and glittered. George could see each fine line around Mr. Clarence's troubled eyes, the grains of his slender fingernails as he clutched a rope, the cracks in his old leather boots as the two balanced on the deck of a schooner floating in the middle Atlantic.

By then there had been no land for two weeks. Mr. Clarence spent the days sitting upon his folding stool on deck with his Bible, out in the wind and glare, while George stared over the rail at the water. The deep blue of the sea stretched to the rim of the world and hazed into the bleached blue of the sky. It was peaceful, George thought, mineral and quiet, and he passed the days watching for the creatures that sometimes let themselves be seen. A ray with shadowy, undulating wings an arm's depth in clear water; a sea turtle with leather flippers plying the surface, its beaked head straining up to see; a Portuguese man-of-war, its pink crest sailing above the blue globe of its body. To George, who had seen only seagulls, apple trees, and sheep, these creatures seemed the strange, ancient counterparts of those wild plants on the dock.

A wandering albatross once flew around the ship. From wing to wing it was broader than George was tall, and he sat with his burnt arms wrapped around his knees and squinted up as the cool shadow ran over his skin. The bird's eye glanced down at him. And in that moment he had a sensation, quick as light, that he glimpsed a different world: a world much older than the one Mr. Clarence's God had created.

They reached the archipelago at dawn. First they saw nothing but a dull cloud upon the water. As the sun rose and they sailed nearer, this gave way to mountainous shapes, hints of green and brown that gradually grew dense, until all at once the place was real. Three mountain peaks rose up, the tips lost in cloud, the moisture of the air clustering about them just as the crashing surf formed a white ring along the coast.

"Volcanic," Mr. Dunn said, as the three stood at the rail. "Two of the mountains only recently formed. Their substance isn't even stable but a crumbly pumice that tumbles free at a jab. There are other peaks that vanished almost as soon as they rose."

Mr. Clarence and George peered at the place.

"And stricken by earthquakes," said Mr. Dunn. "In 1522, again in 1630, and I wouldn't be surprised if another weren't in store. Otherwise, though, as the guidebooks say, were these islands embellished by civilized life, they'd be a terrestrial paradise."

The sides of the mountains were riven with dark gullies; waterfalls fell without a sound. Then, mingled with the salt of the air, drifting over the crashing waves out to sea was the faint, sweet fragrance of orange blossoms.

THEY SAILED ALONG the southern coast until, at dusk, they reached the principal town. It was dense with colored and white buildings, small conical hills behind them, crisscrossed with walls enclosing groves. That evening, as the ship rocked, the air was pierced with the strange cry of an unfamiliar gull, its call between that of an infant and something primordial. As darkness fell, the cries filled the night air, mollusks glowed violet in the black water, and Mr. Clarence looked in silence at the corner of Creation where they'd washed up, while George stared at this new land as the first man might have done.

3

An American named Mr. Furnell, whose property bordered Mr. Clarence's, met them at the dock. He was a small man with lightless hair but sharp eyes, and he looked around pleased at the crates of oranges and lemons surrounding them as they waited for their chests. "A good season," he said. "Your vessel was here earlier with the lumber for the crates— it comes from the Portuguese mainland—and now she's back for the harvest."

Mr. Furnell raised himself up on his toes, gazing at the bustle. "But you'll soon know all about our world of citrus. Your groves aren't as bad off as they look; you'll have little trouble setting them right, the conditions are so good. And you've got that undeveloped plot outside the groves, where you could even extend—"

"Yes, I don't know," said Mr. Clarence, squinting in the brilliant light.

"Of course not," said Mr. Furnell. He looked at Mr. Clarence, at his wide gray hat and dusty coat, and up at wavering George, as the trunks were loaded into wagons.

The streets were narrow and roughly paved, crowded with bullock-drawn carts that had large wooden wheels bound with iron, their screech searing the air. Lining the streets were stalls of fish, poultry, eggs, oranges, lemons, and strange fruits that Mr. Clarence and George peered at. Maracuja, said Mr. Furnell; cape strawberry, custard apple, pimentão, all introduced from Africa, from Brazil. Astounding, he said, what could be got these days.

Everywhere were dogs, asses, and pigs, boatmen in scarlet caps, women in indigo cloaks with peaked hoods. Priests in black petticoats carried green umbrellas against the winter sun; nuns sat in the shade making bouquets from exotic feathers. Bells rang from churches and convents.

They traveled by mule, animals pulling the wagons behind. Outside town, the road was bordered by high walls of rough volcanic stone, at the tops of which plants stirred, larger than plants had seemed before.

"No roads have been cut through the interior," said Mr. Furnell. "A new place, only settled by the Portuguese for a few hundred years. And before that, empty."

Mr. Clarence looked at him. "Empty?"

"Well, except for the trees and bats. But no natives to clear off, no bother. And you've heard of our famous volcanoes?"

The road wound high along the coast toward the eastern tip of the island; sheep grazed on the green hillsides to the left, while to the right, cliffs dropped to the sea. The cliffs were black, the rocks and sand below black as well, and against them the ocean's wild surf broke, flecks of white foam scattering. The blue water stretched away to a haze, and above was the huge open light of the sky, clouds drifting across, their shadows on the sea's glinting surface.

The men paused to rest and look out. Open ocean seen from such a height was dizzying. The huge rock masses of the cliffs looked like black liquid flowing around vast yellow stone that jutted up from the bottom of the sea. It all seemed so freshly cut, so newly made, it was hard for George not to picture the violence.

THE REST OF THE JOURNEY was inland, through wooded ravines, along a narrow path crowded with faya, laurels, and bilberry. Ferns hung from the dripping mountain wall at one side; at the other, wet greenery fell to a gully. The men crossed a stream on an unsteady bridge, then descended into a valley with a lake at its center. On the opposite shore rose smoke.

As they followed the edge of the lake, the air became sulfurous, steam billowing into the trees. In it George could see an old man bending to pull a pot from the ground, a few cows standing in spray. The smell was overpowering, the yellow earth belching like porridge. Sinter coated the path, ferns and leaves starting to petrify.

"Like Hell itself," whispered Mr. Clarence.

Mr. Furnell laughed. "I'd call it a gift. They drop yams in the ground to bake them; the cows rid themselves of vermin. Lots of healing elements in the hot springs. It'll be a handsome industry someday, just waiting to be exploited."

One stream was blood colored, another flowed yellow, and a spray of hot water jetted from a cliff, filling the air with steam.

THE VILLAGE WAS just several rude buildings, beyond which lay the plantations. Mr. Furnell lived in a white raised cottage with a columned porch set deep in foliage; Mr. Clarence's house, not far away, had a latticed veranda and Moorish balconies above. It was spare, and his writing desk and trunks of books did not make it less so, with no carpets and nothing soft but a thin, narrow bed.

George would live in a cottage on the grounds. Its dirt floor, worn smooth by years of treading bare feet, was strewn with green rushes. In the main room was a door but no windows. Chickens and pigs and pigeons had lived there; the place still had their smell. But faya boughs decked the walls, so that, with the rushes upon the floor, the place was softened, more living than stone. Behind a screen of reeds, a staircase led to the bedroom. The bed, stuffed with corn husks, moss, and fern, smelled earthy and dry. It rustled beneath George's heavy body, and the darkness behind his shuttered eyes sparkled with all that he'd seen.

4

MR. CLARENCE AND GEORGE set out before dawn to inspect the orange groves. The moist earth yielded to their boots, and humid air veiled them, sea air that no one had breathed, drifting for miles over the blue. Lichen grew along tree trunks and branches.

The walls of the groves were high to shield the trees from the wind, and within the walls stood another leafy wall of faya, cedar, and fern. The grove itself was ancient, some gnarled trees a century old. They had been planted in quincunx patterns, but years of neglect had obscured the lines. Branches had broken, some from heavy fruit, others from rot, and they lay on the ground, decomposing.

George and Mr. Clarence paced out the groves, shaking their heads and grunting at all the work to be done. George fingered broken branches and spongy trunks. They inspected the sheds, the rusted hoes and shovels.

Mr. Clarence shut his eyes. "A ruin."

When they had finished surveying, they went out beyond the walls to see the plot of undeveloped land. It lay
along a stream that curved, the ground rising to a hillock,
then falling to a cavern. It was deep in ferns and ginger.

"I don't know," said Mr. Clarence. He poked his cane in
the ground. "It's too much to think of what to do here, when
it shall be such a job to restore the groves. We'll let this land
lie." He gazed at the mist hovering in the ferns and put a
hand to his eyes.

"Just a garden," he said softly, after a moment. He looked
up with sudden clarity. "Yes, perhaps just that. A retreat, a
garden." He turned to George. "If we save the groves that's
what we'll do, and retire into it at last."

But George was staring. A garden—it was like the word
was a match that had struck and now the place flared before
him. He *saw* what he wanted. He paced away, heart pounding, up to his chest in ferns. It was confusing, because he suddenly saw all these ferns not as they were but taller and
wilder, as they could be or might once have been—he *felt*
them—he felt trees he had only glimpsed that day on the
dock, with hairy trunks and exotic spiked fronds: he saw all
of this growing up around him in this untouched soil . . .

THEY SET TO WORK on the oranges with a crew of locals, to
whom Mr. Clarence struggled to speak. He had a Portuguese
dictionary in one of his trunks, but he'd never had to say any
of it aloud, and now he spent hours at his writing desk making lists of useful words and practicing them, the sounds
coming monotonous and weird from the echoing room.
Outside, George skeletonized trees, cutting branches back
to the trunk. When the dead wood was hewn and dragged
away, the groves already looked more vital.

Each morning Mr. Clarence put on boots, wielded a

spade, and, joining George, knelt and hacked at the volcanic stone until sweat trickled down his reddened nose, and his old spotted hands were shaking. Then George went over, pulled him up gently, and set him on a chair in the shade.

Mr. Clarence looked down at his dirty hands and wiped them on his trousers. The two men looked around at the place they were in. It was so vivid and intense and *alive*, George thought, the soft earth seemed to be hatching.

TO REPLACE THE TREES that were rotten or damaged, George took shoots from healthy ones, bent them to the ground, and covered them with soil, so that new roots would strike. And this soil made it so easy; it was made of pumice, volcanic ash, and sand, and ran through George's fingers light and clean, free of bones and blood and flesh. When the shoot had developed roots, he cut it away and transplanted it. Soon he had hundreds of new saplings, which he transplanted into holes dug through the crust of a lava field. The lava had tiny vesicles that held trickles of water, so that questing roots could find what they wanted. He protected the young tree at the top of the well with laurel and broom, a miniature enclosure like that of the grove itself within its high walls. When the new tree was strong, he again transplanted it, and in several years, with luck, it would fruit.

Mornings and nights were cool, but as April arrived, the air grew steamy. Blossoms shed their petals and thickened into buds, and the buds gradually swelled.

"A GOOD TREE," said Mr. Furnell, "will produce thousands of fruits a year." He clasped his hands behind his back and pressed the toe of his boot against an orange-tree trunk. "Normally we can expect two thousand, but with one like this, maybe six. But you know it's damned competitive."

When the fruit was still green, men who were called *cabeças* made their rounds for the merchants, sizing up each grove and its potential. *Comprar a fruta no ar,* they called it: buying fruit in the air. They knew all the plantations and could shake branches, cut samples, produce formidable numbers.

But there could be thieves, or storms that would knock the fruit to the ground. And rats that lived high in the trees and scooped out the flesh of an orange, leaving a wafer-thin rind that crushed in the hand. Yet there was hardly an insect in the whole archipelago, and there had never been a blight. Even the death's-head hawk moth, which lurked in shrubs, didn't hurt the trees. And the place had no serpents, no reptiles: too few insects to feed them. Only one mammal had been there when the Portuguese arrived, the bat.

The place was so green, so still and silent and *new.* "Truly something like Eden," said Mr. Clarence.

To George, though, it was different. Eden meant nothing to him. At twilight he roamed through the ferns and ginger in the untouched plot. He heard bats squeaking from the tops of trees and felt the quick beating of ancient wings at his cheeks. If there had been no one on this island, then he stepped upon portions of soil that had never been trod by men. To think of this tree—he placed his large calloused hand upon a trunk—or this stone, which looked as though it had only recently bubbled from subterranean depths and only just cooled and hardened in the air of this world, and to know that both had been here without men: he felt he was drawing nearer.

THE FRUIT SLOWLY swelled, and that year there were no thieves, no bad storms, and few signs of rats. Tiny white-and-purple flowers grew alongside ripe lemons and oranges, bright among the glossy dark leaves.

"And?" said Mr. Furnell, who had come over to see how the first harvest was coming.

Mr. Clarence looked at him.

"Have you tasted one?"

Of course he must taste it, he could not sell it otherwise. He reached up and plucked an orange, like a tiny sun against a dark sea. He held it at the tips of his fingers, then took his knife from his pocket and began to peel. The fragrance sprang up bright and tart as the peel dropped in a coil to the grass. He ate a plump segment.

"So?" said Mr. Furnell.

Mr. Clarence shut his eyes and smiled.

FOR WEEKS the air was full of the shouting and singing of boys in trees, the sawing of wood and hammering of crates, the squealing of wheels on the stony roads. Before all the cottages lay heaps of corn husks, women and children laying them out to dry so the men could use them to wrap each orange. The *cabeças* walked to and fro, supervising, as crates were filled and hooped and bound to mules. Along the coast, ships waited as barges plied between them, laden with crates of fruit.

When the last mule plodded off and the *cabeças* and boys had been paid, the groves fell silent. George and Mr. Clarence stood among the trees; it was late afternoon, light slanting in.

It had all been so easy. Mr. Clarence gazed at the orchards around him with his hands folded upon his cane. He looked as if he could not quite believe he'd washed up in such a place, so new, so vital: precious. He turned to George, face and hair lit. "Now we can make our garden," he said.

And it seemed as though, when it was done, he would go in and lie down and never come out again; he would be gathered in to his final Home.

LATER, FROM THE green cliff, George looked out to sea. It was silent, blue water rippling off until it dissolved into air. Above, the clouds silently drifted.

Far away, a school of porpoises sped in and out of the water. Tiny motion from where George stood, a hunt. Then their speeding stopped and became thrashing, and he could see tiny flashes of silver as fish leapt and struggled to escape. He could feel it, the frantic fight in the water, the bodies torn and falling deep. Yet it was silent, and small, and far.

ACROSS THE SEA to the east just then, the king of Portugal died. So across the sea to the southwest, in Brazil, his son Emperor Pedro became Portugal's king. This didn't please Pedro's younger brother Miguel, who sat nearer the throne than did his tropical brother, who already had an empire. Pedro, though, did not wish to leave Brazil and said he'd place his little daughter on the throne instead. This only angered Miguel more. He began to consider his options.

AND ACROSS SEAS all around the globe, settling and clearing continued; civilization kept advancing. In Tasmania, white settlers at that moment were staking an Aboriginal woman to the ground because, they said, she'd betray them to the blackfellas. Soon she'd be slit from throat to crotch, her innards lying beside her.

In North America, Lakota children were burning alive in a storehouse, their fat dripping upon potatoes that had been stored in the cellar and which now likewise roasted. This made them, the settlers later found, remarkably flavorful.

5

A GARDEN. To wish to make one was easy, but to stand before all that heavy land and fathom how to fill it with life: that was more. So, as George worked in the groves, uprooting saplings or planting new ones or skeletonizing old trees, Mr. Clarence would come out with his stool, stick, *Curtis's Botanical Journal,* and books, and read aloud about gardens so they could decide what to do.

In France, he told George, they manipulated nature, clipping shrubs into the shapes of women or urns and clearing avenues through forests. But in England, they tried to *re-create* nature, building a hillock for a view, encouraging a stream to snake through a meadow. The trouble lay in determining what nature really *was.* How could you change or re-create it otherwise?

"What is natural, they mean," said Mr. Clarence. "What is native. From *natus,* how it was born."

George pondered this. He stopped digging a moment

and looked down at himself: his long shaggy arms, his dirty hands sticky with sap, his large feet sunk in soft volcanic soil on an island in the middle of the Atlantic, having no idea how or where he was born, never having even thought about it.

Even topiary, Mr. Clarence now said, was an idea of nature. Because one meaning of *nature* was like *essence*—the nature of the thing, its purest form. To express the true nature of the yew or hornbeam was to clip it back to the cube or globe hidden within.

But if a yew didn't grow naturally as a cube, how could it be natural? This sort of form dwelled only in the mind of man, and there was no more filthy den.

"Something more clearly natural seems better," said Mr. Clarence. He turned pages and paused at an engraving. "Here, for instance: serpentine lines."

So, as George mended boughs and transplanted saplings, he learned about formal gardens, landscape gardens, serpentine lines, and nature. Looking over Mr. Clarence's bent shoulders and listening to his words drift through the orange trees, he learned about elaborate waterworks, how ladies in silk were driven, laughing, from one pebbled quadrant of shrubbery to another while sprays of water pursued them. He learned about pleaching, espalier, knots, parterres, palisades, and *berceaux*. At night, in his bed of ferns and corn husks, George dreamt of wandering in mad gardens. He ran in terror from a watery serpent that chased him through woods and green mazes.

"But George," said Mr. Clarence as the two stood on the hillock looking out at the plot, "what do you think? You are the gardener, after all."

So George took the journals and writing papers from Mr. Clarence's stool. He knew which pages showed some of the plants he wanted, and he turned to them, breathing hard. He couldn't draw but he tried, a fast wild sketch of the stream and gorge, of palms—he pressed the papers back into Mr. Clarence's hands and moved about, pointing.

"A garden running free into the landscape," said Mr. Clarence. He looked around, nodding, as if he could see it, and again at the pictures George had showed. "Full of exotics . . . A sort of Noah's Ark of a garden." He studied George, and his face slowly lit. "Yes," he said, "why not? Given the wonders that plant collectors are finding these days! It could be a memorial to—all of God's Creation."

Mr. Clarence soon learned that an estate on Terceira, the next island, had introduced cactuses, dragon's blood, figs. So what might naturally grow there, might make itself at home?

Palms, thought George. He still couldn't understand how he had felt when he saw one, its long, thin trunk, the abandoned fronds tossing against the sky, exotic and wild. And the monkey puzzle tree, sharp-spined and erect, its arms whorling out, as much animal as plant, and the tree fern, so ancient that even the sunlight falling through its tender green fronds seemed purer, warmer, from another time.

A park of wild, primordial trees! George could see it as he paced through the ferns and ginger. It hovered, dark and breathing, around him. Men might bend and weave branches to form fanciful tree houses, but now he knew that there were single trees that became whole forests, their long branches reaching out and then dropping to grip the earth with muddy fingers, making shaggy, woody rooms. Genuine grottoes, not contrived. There were ferns as tall as trees, and wild pale things with pendulous fruits, and palmlike trees that walked over the ground . . . And these were what he wanted, this was the place that stirred to life inside him.

He had once seen something like it: high on a grassy

moor in the Hebrides stood a mammoth petrified forest. Stone trees jutted like huge teeth from the top of a cliff, permanent, ancient, unconcerned. This was what he pictured, but *alive.*

For to George the garden seemed not a creation but a fact, something that had existed once and was now forcing its way back up through deep cracks.

"You feel some sort of *kinship* to exotics, don't you," said Mr. Clarence, as George stared down at engravings of newfound plants, his hands and face black with volcanic soil.

"But do you know," Mr. Clarence went on pensively, leafing through articles, "Linnaeus tells us that the country of palm trees was Man's first abode. That is perhaps where we'd find Eden."

WHEN THE CITRUS TREES flowered, the washerwoman scattered orange blossoms in the linen, and the poultry man brought eggs each day in a basket lined with petals. As flowers turned into tiny fruits, honeysuckle bloomed, and wild fuchsia, and lupine. Among the trees darted canaries and little black birds called *touto negros;* in the woods were red-legged partridges, woodcock, and quail.

George and Mr. Clarence dined on dishes made from the fruit: scallops with orange; pickled lemons; orange flower salad; lemon sandwiches; lime soufflé; tangerine ice. The plantations produced not only the famed Saint Michael's orange, but Sevilles as well, although most were allowed to fall to the ground as they were too bitter for eating, and unusually sweet lemons and limes prized for their odd fragrances. Bergamots grew, as did citrons, tangerines, mandarins, and pommelos. The Valencia orange had been introduced but lost its distinctive flavor, becoming identical to the local fruit. "Maybe elements in the soil," said Mr. Clarence.

As the day progressed and George moved about the groves, taking cuttings and inserting them in neatly sliced stems, or trimming long tips so that the tree would be bushier, Mr. Clarence considered different specimens in his *Curtis's*. Absently he would turn on his stool in accordance with the sun. He would reach up and poke among the leaves for an orange, pluck one, gaze at its bright dimpled skin, draw his knife from his pocket, and peel. When he ate, he shut his eyes, and as he placed each segment upon his tongue, it quivered in anticipation of the burst of tart juice. Between the silent delectation and the slow turning, by day's end he was surrounded by small planetary heaps of peel.

After Mr. Clarence wandered back through the groves to his house, George looked at a journal he'd left behind in the grass. A watercolor of a cabbage palm, a naked woman, an island. And on the next page, an engraving of a fossil, a bone. "The new science of Geology will surely be a potent aid to faith," he read, "exalting our conviction of the Power of the Creator . . ." He tucked the journal under his arm and scooped up the orange peel and took it away, because this soil didn't need fertilizing. All he added was a little lupine, which he took care to allow none of the cows near. For they could not resist the stuff and would eat to excess, to death.

6

WHAT SORT OF garden do you have in mind?" said Mr. Furnell. He and Mr. Clarence sat on his veranda sipping lemonade and rum, while George shuffled in the trees.

"Oh, the details aren't settled," said Mr. Clarence. "But a refuge, a sort of haven."

"Well this is the place for it, out in the middle of nowhere." Mr. Furnell leaned forward and swirled the leaves in his drink. "I'll tell you what interests *me*. These plant-exchange points, these what do you call them, entrepôts. You've got them now in Calcutta, Trinidad, Cape Town, all over. The most valuable plants of each colony are held there, ready for shipping wherever the Empire wants them."

Mr. Clarence lightly touched his ear. "And what sorts of plants are they?"

Mr. Furnell put down his drink. "Useful ones. I'm not talking about flowers. New types of cotton, dyeing plants, drugs. Economic plants, I mean. The point is: just look at our soil and climate; you've seen how things can grow. And our location—right on the trade routes between Europe, Africa, the Caribbean. Consider it! If we put our minds to it we could achieve God only knows how profitable an industry. And we could do even more. Why not plant sugar? That's one good thing about these islands being Portuguese: they're not subject to your British laws against slavery, which will ruin the West Indies planters, you know, throw the whole market to Brazil. So given our proximity to Africa, you see what a chance—"

Mr. Clarence's neck had gone red, and he shook his head quickly. "No," he said, "not at all what we want." He nodded good evening and hurried down the wooden steps, away with George into the orange trees.

As GEORGE TURNED SOIL in the fresh plot of land, Mr. Clarence made lists of what they might have. He held up the pictures for George to see.

The Norfolk Island pine, for instance, which had first stirred Britain's interest in Australia—excellent timber for ship masts, they thought. But to find wood supple enough for just seven spars, thirty trees had to be felled, most being too brittle. "Terrible, such giants felled for naught," said Mr. Clarence. In the engraving, the stumps were like headless men. And the eucalypts, the baobab, the curious she-oak. It looked like a huge bird with drooping green arms. *Casuarina* was her proper name, for she was like a cassowary bird: exotic, said Mr. Clarence, but in a sweet, homely way.

He turned pages, from print to print. "Remarkable. Here's a palm called a fishtail, and one called a lady palm— we could have a whole *tribe* of palms nodding their frondy heads about us . . ."

He turned pages still, from print to print, and paused

now at one that showed no exotic but a small creature embedded in stone. For a moment he read, then shook his head slightly, and turned the page again.

Occasionally he reached up for an orange. But by now he had a habit common among the locals: having plucked a fruit, he glanced to see which side had ripened in the sun. And he only ate that part, the rest now dull in contrast. He smiled a little as he wiped his chin, and tossed the uneaten fruit into the trees.

When he had nodded to sleep, his chin crumpled at his chest, George looked quietly over his shoulder at the pages lying open in his lap. A picture of the earth itself cut open, layers around layers like the rings of a tree, fire glowing at its belly.

MR. CLARENCE AND GEORGE ordered their plants, things with names like *Dicksonia antarctica, Phoenix reclinata, Howeia belmoreana*. The common names being: eucalypts, banksias, she-oaks, tree ferns, palms, both pinnated and fan; traveler's-trees, magnolias, baobabs, catalpas. The names meant little to George, though; he saw the creatures whole. The tree fern with light shining through its green ostrich feathers; catalpas with huge heart-shaped leaves and dangling beans; a palm with a gleaming ebony trunk, swaying against the hot blue sky: all of them in the warm, yellow light, breathing forth a primeval air never breathed by men.

Sometimes George actually had to make himself remember, had to look down at his chest, squeeze his fists, and lift his stiff, mud-caked knees, to recall that he was one of them.

"Yours would be an Eden without man, wouldn't it?" said Mr. Clarence, pondering George one day as the huge man stepped quietly behind a pommelo when Mr. Furnell approached on the path.

Mr. Furnell looked at them both and stifled a yawn. "In

any case," he said, "let me know what you learn about trees. I'm interested in timber."

GEORGE BEGAN TO lay out the garden, drawing long lines in the earth and placing stones for different trees. Palms among tree ferns; banyans with room to drop their shaggy arms and form creeping jungles; giant gunneras along the stream; ferns blanketing the ground. He pictured the plants traveling from New Zealand or Brazil, crossing the oceans, sailing over the equatorial line. He saw supple stems bending from the pots on deck in search of the shifting sun, leaves shuttering themselves to the strange new air, roots touching tentative at unknown soil. He stood sometimes in a spot designated for a particular tree, shut his eyes, and felt the breeze and the light, making sure the place would do. He almost felt himself growing, feet slinking into the soil, arms long and imbued with a sinewy sensibility he could feel but not understand.

George worried as they waited: sea spray, neglect, the blazing sun, waves sloshing over the decks, shipwreck. There could be squalls, doldrums, or wandering waterspouts. The plants were to be carefully packaged: seeds bedded in sand or brown sugar, coated with wax or resin, or sealed in bottles, while bulbs traveled loose in baskets. Living plants were set in moss-lined casks with holes at their bottoms. But what was moss or sugar against the ocean? And if there was not enough sun or fresh water? If they were becalmed?

IN SPRING, the washerwoman once more sprinkled petals in the linens; the poultry man delivered eggs nested in blossoms. Gradually boughs became heavy with fruit the trees seemed so eager to bear. Mr. Clarence still reached up often to pluck an orange and, hardly looking, revolved the little globe to the sun side and peeled just that portion. But after only a segment, he considered the fruit upon his palm and ate no more.

"I wonder," he began. He turned to George. "Just think, how nice a sweet Saint Michael's would be if blended with a bitter Seville."

A perfect orange—what a fine thing to make. His own modest piece of husbandry, an offering to God's grand Creation.

George knew how to do this. He cut away the stem of one fruit tree at a sharp angle, slicing again upward a little way from the cut. This stem he inserted into one from the other sort of tree, so that the two would marry. He bound the juncture with twine and sap. And he was glad to do this for Mr. Clarence, but all the same he was uneasy, because he had never before tried to create a new fruit.

BY THIS TIME, across the sea in Portugal, Miguel had done some thinking. His brother Dom Pedro, emperor of Brazil and abdicator of the Portuguese crown, was very far away. And Pedro's daughter Maria, who wore the crown, was still a child. In a stroke Miguel could remove that colonial Pretender and his child and burn the absurd Liberal Constitution Pedro had foisted upon them. He could reinstate absolute monarchy.

It was easy for Miguel to pull off his coup. By spring he was declared Absolute King, and the *Miguelismo* began.

At once revolts broke out among those who believed in Pedro, Maria, and the Liberal cause. When news of the coup reached the Azores, the citizens declared Miguel a usurper and swore their allegiance to Pedro. Revolt!

Miguel took the news coolly. The resistance itself could be crushed, but this particular location troubled him: the archipelago lay between Portugal and Brazil, an easy rallying point for Pedro should he come to avenge his daughter's ravaged rights. Miguel ordered a flotilla of men-of-war out to punish.

7

MR. FURNELL RUSHED OVER with the news. "Of all the places in the world," he said, waving the paper as he reached the veranda, "you find yourself in a bastion of Liberalism! Miguel's fleets will be here any day, but watch how we destroy them."

George stood tall as a bear by the steps, blood already pounding in his skull, as far out at sea the sails of Miguel's fleet were billowing and three thousand soldiers sharpened blades and readied cannons.

Mr. Clarence took George's arm. "Don't worry," he whispered. "It will all happen on Terceira. It won't come here."

Yet George could see in his eyes that he didn't believe it himself, a glazed look that it was all happening again.

THEN, FIFTY MILES of seawater away, Miguel's men-of-war arrived—eighty gunships, four brigs, and three frigates, a total of three hundred and fifty guns, plus armed transports and more than three thousand troops. Only five hundred Liberal fighters were there to resist them, stationed in the cliffs. Miguelist soldiers splashed up to the sand, but from the forts they were easy targets. Balls whistled through the air, blowing off arms and heads, bayonets plunged into bellies and throats. The Liberals threw boulders, crushing skulls and shattering spines. By seven o'clock those who had survived staggered back to their boats. More than a thousand men had been killed, the sand muddy with blood.

In the quiet volcanic valley, though, you might not know this. Steam drifted up, leafy boughs rustled. The air was full not of the burn of gunpowder or the screams of men or the smell of blood and vomit, but with fragrant citrus and the voices of boys in trees and the creaking of wagon wheels. But Mr. Clarence looked sickened, subdued, and rocked on his stool. And George's head was so full—the ax sinking, her head falling in the snow—that he could hardly see as he plunged his shovel into the soil.

At last Mr. Furnell came with the news: the carnage was over; Miguel's flotilla had been driven back.

"How about that," he said. He paced a line in the grass. "The first Portuguese territory to side with Liberalism! A blow against the Old World. Progress, Mr. Clarence."

THEN IT WAS truly quiet. The trees drew up liquid, absorbed light, and readied themselves to form flower and fruit, while the brothers on either side of the sea just as quietly prepared for war.

"Mr. Furnell calls it Progress," Mr. Clarence said to George. "Yet it all seems to blur with destruction . . ."

Curtis's and the other journals continued to come, and Mr. Clarence pushed the spectacles to the bony bridge of his nose and tried to face the situation. Articles documenting

Civilization, the Empire's advance upon the globe: what men, he said, were making of Creation. Often he looked up at George, his watery eyes baffled. "All the ruin," he said.

George looked over his shoulder. There was an engraving of Australia, and the clearing the settlers did. But the land was bald, all stumps. When the continent Cook and Banks had found was *new!* The colonials fought off both native trees and natives; they girdled the old eucalypts and left them to die, making room for sheep.

And another picture, a gully dense with tree ferns. Someone had done a fine painting, reproduced in color. But men rooted those sentient-looking tree ferns up and swung them over their shoulders like brides, leaving the gully ravaged.

And the mighty mountain ashes in Victoria, more than a thousand years old but chopped down all the same . . . And the petrels on Norfolk Island, birds that saved the colonials from starving, until there was no more fear of starving, but the men, finding they could catch the things by the thousands, grew so perverse they only ripped out the eggs and threw the bleeding birds to the ground.

Mr. Clarence's breath became shallow as he turned pages, and he shut his eyes and pressed his fingers to his lids.

"Sometimes," he said, "I think there will be a new Flood."

He opened his eyes again fast. "No," he said, "not that." He looked away then toward the plot for the garden. And George could see how the old man longed to be finished, to be plucked from this troubling world, to be Home.

EVER SINCE GEORGE had grafted together the two citrus trees, Mr. Clarence had gone each morning to visit them—as if they were his children, his only gift to the green world. He sometimes still plucked a Saint Michael's orange or tangelo, but his eyes drifted hopefully to the new trees. They had recovered from their wounds and seemed fresher and younger than the others, more supple. Mr. Clarence peered into the foliage and felt behind leaflets for tiny buds. The trees all around them broke into bud, and still these did nothing. Yet they looked so lustrous that surely their fruit must be exemplary, he said.

The season advanced. The other trees blossomed, the petals fell to the ground, and hard fruitlets formed in their place; but on the new trees the leaves just grew more waxy and lustrous. Finally it was clear that they wouldn't bud that season.

Mr. Clarence was disappointed, but he patted George's arm. "Ah well," he said. "Next year."

MEANWHILE, their plants were sailing from Australia and Brazil, and would soon arrive on the ships that brought timber for packing the citrus and the journals and books Mr. Clarence made himself read. Not just Civilization but Science pressed on, discoveries involving fossils, geology, new knowledge of the earth. George looked over his shoulder as the old man peered down at these unsettling new mysteries, now an engraving of a deep section of earth with layers of petrified life. Again Mr. Clarence looked as he had in the wagon, as though the world was flying by too fast.

One day he wandered over to George, unsteady in the glaring light. He wiped his face with a handkerchief.

"I've just read something," he said. "Someone, a Mrs. Mantell, has unearthed some unusual teeth."

Papers about these teeth were making their way around scientific circles. They were extremely large, herbivorous teeth that did not belong to any living creature or to anything that much resembled one: they seemed to belong to something altogether *new.*

"New," said Mr. Clarence, "yet somehow extremely old. Really, impossibly old. Older than—anything could be."

Suddenly he shivered in the warm yellow light, and drew his coat close. As if a shadow had just brushed him, or the world. After a moment, he tucked the journal under his arm and wandered off into the trees.

But when he had gone, George stared into the dense black soil. He placed his huge palms side by side on the earth. Large teeth that belonged to no living creature . . .

Digging right here the other day, he had unearthed part of a gigantic, ancient tree that had almost turned to stone. He had felt queasy, crouching in the soft mud at the top of this tree. But consoled, too, as by finding something familiar that had been lost for such a long time. As if the ground itself was offering up hope that the world he so longed for would be true.

ON THE SHIPS that brought the timber for packing the citruses now came Liberal émigrés fleeing the Terror Miguel unleashed in Portugal. Lawyers, poets, doctors, scholars: a handful arrived on every ship. And with them, too, came George's plants. The first batch landed at the harbor and were brought by mule to the valley, and one morning there they were, on the muddy path.

George unwrapped the packages carefully; with shaking fingers he undressed the spiky arms of his first monkey puzzle, a little araucaria from Chile. He smelled it before he felt it, sharp. It sagged but was healthy enough, its branches still green. A dozen palms and tree ferns came potted in moss and were already as tall as young boys; and cycads, bananas:

just seeing them standing all around him, loosening their fronds or floppy leaves in the air, George could see his primal garden, his face brushed by tender green tips.

He placed the new plants in the earth, and they took to it naturally, soon at home in the foreign air. Slowly they unfurled, primeval sunlight filtering through green fans, spikes, and leathery leaves. Sometimes George lay in the ferns and looked up, stretched out his arms and legs and opened his mouth, so that he too would be drenched with sunlight and rain, he too would sprout roots and grow.

8

I AM DAMNED CURIOUS to know what takes," said Mr. Furnell. He and Mr. Clarence were walking up the gravel path through the garden, and he glanced at the fragile new plants staked in place, the fiddleheads slowly uncurling, the mounds of dark soil harboring seeds.

"The trees, I mean," he said. "The way matters are going, we may need to start timber plantations for the crates."

George looked up from transplanting a gunnera into a hole by the stream.

"You think it will go on?" said Mr. Clarence.

"Certain. Pedro's struggling in Brazil; he won't last there, and his daughter's rights have been trampled in Portugal—he can't put up with that. You've seen how our islands are filling with Liberals. Geographically, we're caught between brothers, but politically, we're with Pedro. He'll abandon Brazil and reclaim the old kingdom, and he'll launch his war from here. Then Miguel will cut our lumber supplies; and with no lumber, no crates; and no crates, no orange exports. Anyway, we're fools not to control the industry ourselves, to have this fine land"—he spread his arms, glancing at George as he patted the soil—"and not plant something of *use.*"

"Please don't worry," said Mr. Clarence when Mr. Furnell had gone. "Pedro might not leave Brazil. And if he does— there are other islands. And it will all take a long time."

But Mr. Clarence didn't look as if he believed his own words. He walked back to the groves, whispering to himself, cheeks flushed. His experimental orange trees were now heads taller than the others. He grasped a bough, shook it, and peered into the greenery, but still there was no flower.

Maybe they just weren't ready. But for a while he gazed, lightly touching his ear, as if for the first time he wondered whether what he and George had done might not have been right.

FROM THEN ON, Mr. Furnell appeared regularly at Mr. Clarence's estate to report on the escalating conflict between the two brothers and Dom Pedro's own troubles in his tropical empire. He paced the soft, muddy paths, studying George's young trees as if he would seize them, while Mr. Clarence glanced through the fans and ferns as if soldiers already approached.

"I wish Pedro would just leave it be," he burst out.

Mr. Furnell laughed and cracked his knuckles. "And allow a usurper, a rotten monarchy in Portugal? Men demand progress and *improvements,* Mr. Clarence. I'd think you as a Briton would know that. What with the advances the British have brought to Australia, to India—"

Mr. Clarence was breathing hard. "Those are scarcely improvements," he whispered.

Mr. Furnell stared at him. "Of course they are. The advance of Empire. From woods to pastoralism to agriculture to commerce: the natural course of man's dominion."

"Not," said Mr. Clarence, "if things are lost—"

"Lost? Rather, gained! Good God, Mr. Clarence—"

And George saw again the bleeding birds with their eggs ripped out, the severed ancient trunks, the disemboweled gully, the woman staked to the grass and slit open, the soldiers stringing people's heads on a rope . . . His head pounded and he hurried away to his park.

After a time in the airy, shadowy grounds, he grew calm. He could almost hear his plants growing, the trees pulling themselves from the soil, turning water and light into trunk. He could already see the Brazilian gunnera's voluptuous, umbrellalike leaves filling the stream, see the Australian tree ferns grow tall and plume out, light falling through their feathery heads; the needling fronds of the cycads uncurling, their dense yellow cones pushing through; the bananas casting up their huge abandoned leaves, the fruit dropping in bunches and dangling heavy red flowers. All of it seemed his element as he strode through the warm oceanic air, his feet sinking into the volcanic soil, his long bones stretching. It seemed that he was finally near it, the original place, the untouched place, the place where he belonged.

But if men came, and war, and timber . . .

His newest tree was young, but soon its roots would be like huge dark serpents snaking over the ground. They would form leathery crests as high as his shoulder and would creep and twine twenty paces away; the branches were like sinewy arms that would drop to the ground and clutch and form new trunks, until the tree itself had become a forest, forbidding, impenetrable by men. And that was all he wanted.

By now the fruit season had nearly ended, and still the new trees hadn't budded. Mr. Clarence inspected them each morning, while George followed slowly, knowing nothing was there.

Such lush foliage, so sterile! Mr. Clarence laughed a little, but his face gazing up at the trees was worried.

Mr. Furnell had come over, as always. He pretended to amble about the garden, but George saw him secretly measure a monkey puzzle and even put his boot to the trunk of a tree fern. Then he went to the groves and watched Mr. Clarence poke his new citruses for signs of fruit.

"Well," said Mr. Furnell after a time, "if it's a new orange you're wanting so badly, in Florida they're growing one they claim is better than ours. The *original* orange, they call it. Some rigmarole about Ponce de León and the land of the Fountain of Youth."

Mr. Clarence glanced over. "Original orange?"

Mr. Furnell yawned. "And Fountain of Youth. If you believe that sort of thing. It's the land of the Seminole Indians, too, who've been making things damned hot for Jackson. But now the vermin have been cleared away, so planters are going in to cultivate."

Mr. Clarence looked at him. "Vermin?"

"Seminoles, I mean."

Mr. Clarence gave a little laugh.

Mr. Furnell looked at him and laughed as well. "What, again? Against civilization and improvements? My God, Mr. Clarence. Don't you know that *you*, too—"

But he stopped. He shook his head at the older man and smiled.

Mr. Clarence looked back at him, his blue eyes flecked with doubt.

9

JUST AS MR. FURNELL predicted, Pedro finally abandoned his tropical empire. He abdicated the throne to his five-year-old son, who, after all, was a native Brazilian. He himself would go reclaim the Portuguese crown, which his brother had stolen.

MR. CLARENCE sat down heavily on his stool when he heard. "But surely he will not come *here*."

"Surely he will, Mr. Clarence!"

"To Saint Michael? Not Terceira, where so many Liberal supporters have gathered—"

"Oh no. Oh no. Much better here, given our size and position to the east. A perfect launching point for his war."

PEDRO ARRIVED on the first day of Carnival, at dawn. From his ship he wrote a letter to the Liberals on land, proclaiming himself Regent of Portugal and protector of his daughter's rights. A fisherman rowed it in.

News of Pedro's arrival spread fast. Even in the quiet valley, the excitement could be felt.

"Celebrations all over!" reported Mr. Furnell. "An ancient regime to be toppled! Just as America freed itself from Britain, and Brazil freed itself from Portugal, now Portugal shall rid itself of a dictator. A turn in the revolution of history!"

"But," said Mr. Clarence, "they are *brothers* . . ."

"That doesn't matter to history."

But history, thought George, as he stood swaying with his grimy hands clutching his elbows, what was human history? When beneath all the heads and arms that were soon once more to be crushed into the earth stood mighty forests, preserved in ash spewed from a mountain's bowels?

MR. FURNELL SAID they must take part in so momentous an occasion, so the three men rode mules along the same route they'd followed years before, to witness Pedro's arrival. All along the way water flew through the air. Children ran after them, blowing water through hollow stalks; women appeared suddenly at windows and flung dishwater as they passed, then dissolved into laughter, into darkness.

"Out with the old and in with the new!" cried Mr. Furnell, digging his spurs into the mule. "Carnival and Revolution!"

In town they joined a crowd who had turned out to see Dom Pedro step to shore. The Liberals' officers met him with ceremony, soldiers fired military salutes, a band accompanied the entourage from ship to palace along streets decorated with triumphal arches of orange boughs, the patterned gray paving stones strewn with petals. Generals made speeches and toasts.

"To arms against usurpation!" shouted Pedro. The crowd roared.

Then it was all Revolution and Carnival. Men pelted women with wax lemons that broke in splashes of scent, water snaked through the crowd, people shrieked and beat drums, the iron wheels of carts screamed on the stones, and beyond all this, beyond the hot roofs, the masts and sails of men-of-war and merchantmen jostled in the harbor, fire rockets exploding above them so that the air was as full of smoke and water as noise. Mr. Clarence stood in the shadow of a church, sweat sheening his nose, shielding his eyes with a hand.

"Out with the old and in with the new!" shouted Mr. Furnell again, hurling a lemon. "To Revolution and Progress!"

"Maybe we've seen enough," whispered Mr. Clarence.

He and George turned their mules from the chaos and hurried between high stone walls to the open fields, the road that wound along the coast. They paused on a bluff and looked out at the gleaming blue Atlantic. The day was clear, the sky full of light, the black cliffs melting and flowing.

The two gazed down at the liquid rock and rough yellow boulders being battered by waves. Mr. Clarence fixed his stick in the ground and rubbed his eyes. He looked at his hand then, the fine web of skin between finger and thumb, the thin bones visible. He looked again at the sleek rock, the sloshing sea.

"Hutton and Lyell think the ground is made again and again," he said softly. "Mountains are gradually washed into the sea, and their matter is compressed and melted deep in the earth, and then new mountains are cast up elsewhere." He shook his head and turned away. "That is awfully hard to grasp. It would simply take so much time. No, it goes against—it goes against everything."

He looked weary, and pressed his handkerchief to his forehead. It seemed that they were wavering, precariously high, in the middle of an endless expanse of sea. He fixed his stick more firmly in the ground, but the soil slipped away; the earth they clung to was itself loose and crumbling. The sky opened vast and oblivious all around. Far below, waves broke soundless; the clouds had already changed.

IT WOULD TAKE Pedro several months to raise his army. As he sailed from island to island, enlisting troops, he had the church bells taken down and smelted, then recast as coin to pay the soldiers. Meanwhile the trees that had been in flower when he arrived grew bright with yellow fruit. Boys climbed the branches, and the air rang with the hammering of nails in crates. The timber had come as usual, because war had not yet been declared.

"It will be, though," said Mr. Furnell. "Just wait."

"But surely," said Mr. Clarence to George, "Mr. Furnell is wrong." He looked weary, this world of clearing and conquest and war all so overwhelming. In the garden now he sometimes paused in his slow, careful steps as if he heard someone whispering to him, that Voice gently calling him Home. He spent all his time there, murmuring and touching the tender tips of ferns. He never wanted to leave the garden, even when the sun sank. He said once that he'd like just to go to sleep there, make himself a little bed in the ferns and at last hear that Voice all around.

But surely, thought George, Mr. Furnell was right. He stared from the bluff at the sea full of masts and gray smoke, trailing from steamships. Of course there'd be war. There always was. Men did what they wanted, and they always wanted more.

But with a little luck, he thought then, perhaps they would finally destroy themselves.

WHEN MR. FURNELL came now, he no longer hid what he was after. He stared at a wrapped plant George was lifting from a wheelbarrow. "What in God's name is that?"

"It's marvelous what's possible these days," said Mr. Clarence dreamily, as George freed a baby palm of its sacking. "Gardens in Calcutta, Sydney, Trinidad, and Rio are gathering spectacular specimens. This is a *Howeia forsteriana,* an altogether aboriginal palm, collected in Australia. And that"—he pointed past George to a tiny tree with enormous leaves—"is a Red Indian bean tree from North America. There is even, on Saint Helena island, a convalescent center for plants that have taken ill as they journey between hemispheres. What a fine innovation in botany!"

"You don't say," remarked Mr. Furnell.

Mr. Clarence glanced up, then returned to a page in his journal. "Yesterday we ordered this, a Florida tree that bears crumpled, blood-orange blossoms. Her leaves are bedecked with insects like jewels. Harmless, though ornamental: They derive all their sustenance from her. So we shall gird the park with the snake trees George loves, and at the heart of our garden shall stand a single jeweled tree."

"Ah," said Mr. Furnell. He smiled and looked as if he wanted to say more. "In fact—" he began.

"Yes?" Mr. Clarence looked up and waited.

"In fact, this tree shall be the jewel in the crown."

Mr. Clarence blinked. "I beg your pardon?"

"For God's sake. The jewel in the crown! Like India. The gem of the Empire." Mr. Furnell smiled broadly at Mr. Clarence, who stared back at him without a word.

"Good God, Mr. Clarence. Don't you know what you two do? Call those places what you want, but they're the entrepôts I told you of. And they weren't made for garden lovers like you. It's all about Empire, Mr. Clarence, about getting the resources we need. And we've only just begun to scrape at the Orient, Africa, Australia. Take your garden in Calcutta," he said. "It's a holding pen for the tea taken from China, now that Britain has India and can plant it as she likes. The jewel in the crown, Mr. Clarence. It's all the same enterprise. And all of this—" He laughed and gestured at the exotics. "This is nothing but the Empire's plunder."

Mr. Clarence sat still. His hair seemed very fine in the light, strands dangling before his eyes like cobwebs. George stood behind him, stricken.

Mr. Furnell studied them both, then shrugged and strode among the plants, his boots leaving deep prints in the soil.

"Anyway. Now that war's coming we'll need fast trees. I hear eucalypts are good timber and colonize anywhere. And some kind of sea pine's supposed to be cheap. Casua-, casua-something."

"Casuarina," whispered Mr. Clarence.

"That's the one. Got it?"

"Oh . . ."

When Mr. Furnell had gone, Mr. Clarence sat on his stool, not seeming to see George or the groves around him.

Then he looked up, at the sunlight sifting through a tree fern from New Zealand, at the spiked green arms of a monkey puzzle from Chile.

"All just to interest the plant collectors," he said softly. "Like trinkets dangled before a native, so they plunder well. All hand in glove. So we, too, in our little garden . . ."

He faltered, and his hands fell to his sides.

"We, too, with all the clearings and cruelty . . ."

His thin frame shivered, and he put a hand to his neck. "We are as deep in it as anyone," he whispered. He turned to George, a ring of white around his eyes.

But he said no more, just sat, as if there was no more to say.

After a time he fixed his stick in the ground and struggled to his feet. George took his arm and the two walked home through the trees.

10

AFTER THAT, GEORGE watched Mr. Clarence as he sat pensive among the dark foliage. The older man still glanced up at the oranges and clementines, but he never picked one. He read his books and journals, but what was in them only troubled him, and more and more often his eyes wandered from the page to stare at the exotics in the garden. For spells he sat without moving.

Then he let the books slide from his lap and went through the lemons and tangelos to the new hybrid trees. They flaunted sinewy trunks, glossy leaves, and sharp thorns, but still they didn't flower. It was no longer fruit that he longed to see. He wanted a sign. But he found nothing.

"WE HAVE TAKEN the Falkland Islands," Mr. Clarence said from his cane chair on the veranda, not particularly to George. "One reads that it is surprising the place was not long ago colonized."

For it was wondrous, he read, how Englishmen spread all over the globe, embryo Englands hatching in all parts. On Saint Helena island, every native species had been cleared off and killed, replaced with the familiar shrubs an Englishman likes around him at home.

And in India, in Bangalore, four natives accused of plotting against their English masters were tied to cannon barrels, the fuses were lit, and the men were blown to pieces. A lesson.

"Meanwhile," Mr. Clarence went on, "the extermination of the Pampas Indians continues, so that their lands can be cleared and the fruits enjoyed. Once the mothers are killed, the children can be bought for three pounds sterling."

And the Aborigines of Tasmania, those who hadn't yet been shot, were cleared and shipped to another island, where every one of them perished. The end of a whole race of men. Mr. Clarence stared at the page and began to laugh, his birdlike shoulders shaking.

"We men," he said, "regress. We even become cannibals."

At night George wandered through his primordial park, touching the tips of a lady palm frond, the plush trunk of a tree fern. The hairy stems of the gunneras now rose above his head, the leaves like finely thorned umbrellas, moonlight shining through the veins. The garden was quiet but for the squeak of bats, the creeping of tendrils and green blood. He passed from the park into the orange groves. There he saw Mr. Clarence, among the barren new trees.

The old man turned, naked and ghostly blue in the moonlight. But he said nothing, just stood there wavering.

The hybrid trees continued to grow more vigorous. And one day, buds appeared at the tips of the branches. Delicate flowers soon followed, which gave way to tiny furred fruits.

George examined them but did not yet show them to Mr. Clarence.

It went more quickly than usual, as Mr. Clarence had predicted: these fruits would be exemplary. They shed their down and grew plump, the skin waxy and dimpled.

BY NOW PEDRO had recruited nine thousand men. Fifty warships filled the bay, masts swaying, sails flapping, sailors shouting from the riggings the way boys sang from the branches of trees at harvest. They would attack the mainland near Porto. Miguel would have eighty thousand men to Pedro's nine, but he could not know when his brother would strike.

Just as the fleets were ready to set sail, George came to the grove and found that one of the new oranges was ripe. Not only that: it had sprouted a finger. This poked from the dimpled skin, long and slightly hooked. He stared and didn't touch it.

A few days later, he came again and found an orange with not one finger but two. Then a third fruit appeared, with a tail wound about it.

Finally George had to bring Mr. Clarence to see.

The old man stared at the hideous tree, its leaves so glossy, its thorns so sharp, its fruit like bright deformed children, dangling. He opened his mouth but said nothing, turning to George with panicked eyes. Mr. Furnell looked on with interest and plucked an orange by the tail.

So was it, as Mr. Clarence feared, a sign of God's anger that he, too, had done so much wrong in His garden?

Or was Nature simply sporting, casting up such a fruit?

Or could the fruit in fact mean nothing? No Mind or Hand anywhere, just a result.

AFTER THAT, Mr. Clarence ate little. As he punished himself he became even thinner, his hair floating from his head in stray strands. His gums looked bruised, and his yellow teeth grew brittle and broke; George saw him wipe blood from his lips.

The trees continued to produce oranges with lolling tongues, oranges distended like cucumbers or fingered like hands. George shook them from the trees before dawn, wheeled them to the edge of the grove, and buried them. Then he paced in the garden, his footfalls silent though heavy in the soil. He stopped beneath the tulip tree, at whose crown the small bats fluttered black against the lightening sky. Beneath the tree, the warm stream bubbled.

He thought, the original orange.

He knew by now how to do it. In his cottage in the lamplight, his hand was large and awkward with the feather pen, but he took pains over each letter he printed.

It would be at least a month before they arrived, but maybe within the season he'd have for Mr. Clarence the original orange, the fruit watered by the Fountain of Youth.

II

PEDRO'S FLEETS finally set sail, and the War of the Brothers began. Then, as Mr. Furnell had foretold, shipments of lumber stopped. And just as the monstrous fruits ripened so did all the others—lemons, limes, citrons, clementines, tangerines, and pommelos. The planters didn't know what to do; they'd thought somehow it wouldn't come to this. They waited. Maybe the war would be brief, and the merchantmen would once again appear in the east with the usual loads of timber. But if the war was brief, it would be Miguel who won, and the islands' punishment would continue. Meanwhile the fruit swelled, and the boughs dipped with its weight.

"Just as I said." Mr. Furnell paced up and down his veranda, the heels of his boots hard on the planks. "We're cut off. But our citruses won't slow their ripening for an embargo. I've been planting cheap eucalypts and sea pines, but they'll need another year to be useful; thank God it's crates we need, not masts. We've got to find new sources, and that will take time. Until then we must fell what we have."

So all over the island the trees began to fall—faya, juniper, cedar, laurel, tree-heath. First to go were the most ancient ones around Ribeira Grande, great trees sixty feet high and centuries old. The earth shuddered as the giants crashed to the ground, and grew red and rutted where the huge trunks were dragged off. Even from their secluded valley, Mr. Clarence and George could smell the ruin. The hills rang with the blows of axes.

MR. CLARENCE no longer left his veranda, and now he ate almost nothing—a fish sometimes, maybe a yam. As he read, his eyes became hollow, his veined cheeks more gaunt, as if the words he devoured were consuming him.

One day, in the middle of his reading, he looked up at George. He had just read something, he said. He licked his lips but his mouth was dry, and he sat staring in his cane chair as George fetched him some water.

It seemed, Mr. Clarence said, that the scientific men had finally solved the problem of the teeth Mrs. Mantell found. They were believed to belong to enormous reptiles that once wandered the world. The earth had been these creatures' dominion. And this was a very long time ago, longer than anyone had imagined life possible—unfathomably older than the Bible said life could ever have been. Yet there the teeth were, the creatures themselves lost now, nothing but fossils. Nothing like them still existed.

Mr. Clarence's mouth worked, his fingers clenched.

"What God does endures for ever," he said. *"Nothing can be added to it, nor anything taken from it."*

But either this was wrong, and God made things that could become extinct. Or else these creatures had not been made by God. They had somehow existed without Him. Before Him.

Mr. Clarence looked back at the journal, as if for help. "'There has been,'" he read on, "'a succession of worlds.'"

A succession of worlds . . . He stared at George and continued. "'We find no vestige of a beginning in the earth . . . The very ground remakes itself again and again . . .'"

This would mean, then, no Creation. He laughed a little. Because from there it was the easiest skid to the next thought: that God Himself . . .

Mr. Clarence and George stared at each other. In the skull of the older man, fear pressed deep and cold. You could see, as he sat there, the world sliding away beneath him. He looked around very slowly.

But the same news flamed through George's body. There *had* been a world before men and their God. It had all long existed without them. And like those lizards, men, too, would die off, and the world would shrug and live on.

Mr. Clarence's hands were trembling; he pulled his shawl tighter around his shoulders. "Always chilled," he said.

Turning back into dull matter. But now, with little hope of comfort, of home. Just bones to join other old bones in the soil.

"TAKE HIM TO our hot springs, for Christ's sake," said Mr. Furnell. "The Fountain of Youth's right in the backyard."

So George took Mr. Clarence to the lake and streams. Cows stood placid in the hot sprays as sulfurous steam rose up, making Mr. Clarence's fine hair curl.

The old man lowered himself into the water, his eyes shut. When he was settled, he gripped George's wrist and rocked a little. He let his head fall back, strands of hair floating on the surface. Then he opened his eyes, and, first with just a shake in his thin arms, then with his whole body quaking, he began soundlessly to laugh.

"Bubbles," he said at last, his eyes pink-rimmed and watering. "They rise up from beneath . . . and tickle."

He pulled a hand from the water and ran it over his eyes. Within his skinny ribs it seemed a silent battle raged, like those George had seen from the cliff among the hunting dolphins and the glittering fish. After a time Mr. Clarence stared again, as if he felt himself floating on depths immeasurable and dark.

12

*A*T LAST THE NEW Florida orange trees arrived. George rolled them quickly to the quarter of the groves he'd quincunxed beforehand. Trees from the original orange! Watered by the Fountain of Youth.

Mr. Clarence wouldn't notice them; he never left his veranda and blanket, but sat there looking dully at the greenery, the blackbirds, the empty new world. He wouldn't notice the fragrance of the new blossoms either; it was lost in the perfume that rose from the groves and drifted out to sea.

George visited the new trees every day, saw the slight difference in their blossoms and fruits, and guessed that these would ripen early. Some fruitlets were nearly full in his hand, their color warming from green to yellow.

When the first orange was ripe, George roused the old man.

"What is it?" said Mr. Clarence, groping in the air.

With a blanket around Mr. Clarence's shoulders, George

led him through the dark alleys of leaves to his secret new grove. But when they reached it, the fruit had fallen.

"Ah well," said Mr. Clarence, not noticing that the oranges were different. "Don't worry. A windy night."

But it happened again the next week. Just as two oranges were nearly ready, they fell—and not only fell but were spoiled. When George cut one open, the pulp was brown. But he could find no mildew or parasite or other culprit. Each fruit, seemingly perfect, was rotten inside. At the tips of some shoots glistened dark, viscid drops.

Mr. Clarence tried to comfort him. "You will find a way to cure it. You always do."

But George couldn't. He cut down one of the new trees, dissected its roots and trunk, but he couldn't find the cause.

Then gradually, so very gradually that for a time he didn't see it, the bark of an orange tree bordering the new grove began to fissure. A fine crack grew until a rent ran up the trunk. This widened and split, as the carcass of an animal bursts from the agitation of all the tiny new life inside. From the wound oozed a liquid that on George's finger was sticky and red. When he saw it, his ears roared, the old pain seared his eyes.

But he knew better! It was just an ailment he'd never seen, a *molestia* that could be explained. Something had leached into the soil, or there was some insect, a rot.

But it didn't seem so. It seemed, rather, a curse.

As when an ancient tree was said to have screamed and bled when struck by an ax, and the man wielding the ax, guilty of greed, was infested with hunger that wouldn't be sated until he ate his own hands.

THE *MOLESTIA* spread like slow fire from tree to tree, each one producing rotted fruit and bearing bark that split and bled.

"*Lagrima, lagrima,*" the *cabeças* said, pointing to their weeping eyes.

When it had reached a tenth of their groves, George and the men began to cut trees down. All that were blighted, and all that grew near them. Tree after tree, he swung his ax, sobbing. Dark boughs, white blossoms, oranges fell to the ground.

But even so, the blight spread on. It reached a quarter of Mr. Clarence's groves, then half. They could hardly fell the trees fast enough. Some were two hundred years old, older than colonies, or empires.

A FOREIGN INFECTION? wondered the planters. Because there had never been a blight on the island, or a damaging insect. Surely it had come from outside. Brazil, maybe? Pedro's cargo?

But Mr. Clarence—

When it became clear that this was truly a scourge, he came out to the orange groves in his tattered pajamas and slippers. He took in the fallen trees, the rotted fruit, the withered leaves. But when he saw the scores of rent trunks oozing red liquid, he began to laugh. Quietly at first, then shrill and gasping, he laughed like a madman in the rain. He laughed until his eyes streamed.

Because, he said, of course it was a curse. Anyone looking at it could see.

It was a curse, his punishment.

And this, it seemed, was Mr. Clarence's salvation. For to him it was better, so much better, to be cursed by God and condemned to Hell, than that God should not exist.

HE TOOK TO HIS BED. Eyes shut, mouth open, thin wrinkled arms lifeless on the sheets, while outside, the crack of axes never stopped. Finally George gathered him up in the bed-sheets and carried him through the ruined groves to the hot springs. Once in the water the old man revived a little, flushed spots appearing in his haggard cheeks.

"George." He coughed and cleared the phlegm from his throat. Fine bubbles were breaking on the water's surface around him, and he pointed like a child. "I have been reading of earthquakes. The ground is firm beneath one's feet, then suddenly one tumbles. Cattle roll from cliffs into the sea."

He gazed at George, his eyes bright. "But now I understand. Because here where I sit is the crack that opens down to that violent hot blood. And do you know? I hear him. I hear him waiting to boil me."

"ABEL'S BLOOD in the ground!" he cried at night in a fever.

"But the Pampas women fought fiercely!" he screamed. "They defended themselves with large stones! Oh, but they bred so, what else could we do?

"Because," he cried, his marble eyes open, "we wanted their Golden Apples!"

MR. CLARENCE lay in bed for weeks, his skin waxy, hands curled like claws. Outside, orange trees continued to fall. Not just his but Mr. Furnell's, too, all the groves on the island, until the *molestia* leapt over the water and reached the next island. Everywhere rose the smell of rot. Mr. Clarence shut his eyes, the white lashes trembling.

"Had we not dealt between bark and tree, forbidden mixtures there to see." He looked up and smiled, beatific, toothless.

"I wish—" he began. He giggled. "No."

He gripped George's collar. "Yes," he whispered. "I'm glad I'm going. And I wish we all could be done away with, and this world could start anew."

BY NOW MR. CLARENCE stank of the fruit and lumber rotting outside. Not just the orange trees but the giants, felled for crates that were no longer needed. The islands were fields of stumps.

Mr. Clarence lifted a hand toward George, a hand rivered with veins. "The finest oranges," he whispered, "are barren. Rinds as fine as paper, no pips. They ripen, then nothing. Like me. And I am glad. But you, George, you are not like me, you must—"

He couldn't breathe, just that terrible mouth open.

Finally he said, "In the sea, George. No casket."

AND HE WAS GONE. George stood still, the old hand in his. After a time he placed it on the thin chest, and arranged the other hand upon it for comfort. He gazed down at the sunken cheeks and arched nose in the bare, leafless light.

Then outside, out through the rotting groves, past Mr. Furnell standing among his own ruin, past the hot streams billowing steam and the cool streams smelling of iron, up the muddy hills that had never been tamed and were still dense with ferns, the island's ancient greenery. He climbed and struggled, boots slipping, face slick with sweat. It was a steep climb to the peak, and when he got there he was gasping, his skull full of that pounding, hot blood.

All around the island, the ocean stretched out vast, reflecting the shifting clouds. It was silent. He stood there, up in the open sky, and was stricken with dizziness, with a mortal confusion.

For the first time George understood that he was a *man*, like any, wandering lost upon the earth. Something like homesickness ripped at his chest, as all around the ocean glinted.

13

As if the ruin of the groves had not been enough, the island was struck that night by an earthquake. Even before it began, the air changed, so that all over Saint Michael, dogs quietly got up from their corn husk nests and trotted to the hills. The earth rocked gently at first, then bucked. People screamed, and cows ran with their tails in the air, stumbling and rolling on the heaving ground. George lay in his ruined grove, clutching the volcanic crust as it rocked upon liquid.

But the next morning it seemed that there was little damage, just cracks in pavement, a few walls knocked down. Yet after the tremor a rush of seawater overtook the coast, so high it submerged the nearer cottages. It receded just as fast.

George saw the traces of that tide when he rode to the sea with Mr. Clarence's body, wrapped in linen. Stones had been belched up along the beach, which was coated with ashes and strewn with boiled fish, their eyes blanched and popping. Yet the sea was as calm as if nothing had happened, slight waves breaking upon the shore, glinting with floating fish.

George lowered Mr. Clarence's body into a rowboat, pushed the boat out over the waves, and climbed in. He rowed toward where the explosion had been, the distant point where even now a thin spire of smoke rose from the sea into the sky. After a time he dipped his hand in the water; it was warm.

He drew nearer. There wasn't only smoke but also cinders and stones shooting up from the water and scattering in the sky like black fireworks. Lightning flashed, the air seemed to boom, and warm mist floated from the dark column. Now the water around the boat was hot, smoke roiling beneath the surface.

Yes, Mr. Clarence seemed to say within his swaddling. *Here, George. Hell itself.*

George gathered up the old man and held him on his knees. He kissed his brow, lifted him to the side of the wobbling boat, and slipped him over the side. As Mr. Clarence sank, the linen came loose and unwound, billowing in the smoky water. The pale body sank free into darkness.

GEORGE LINGERED then, the boat bobbing on the sea. He didn't know where to go.

But something seemed to be happening underwater. Between his boat and the black spout, something seemed to be emerging. A glossy ring formed on the water's surface, as when a whale rises. George rowed nearer. Whatever was rising was much bigger than a whale. He rowed along the edge of the ring at a distance, for the water any nearer now steamed and spat. Soon he had rowed a huge circle, and he could see that it was the rim of an enormous crater. In places, it actually broke the surface of the sea; soon it had broken through all around. A rocky wall surrounded a spire of black ash.

George stayed out in his boat that night, warmed by the hot sea, plucking from the water a boiled fish to eat. By dawn the thing had risen to the height of a ship.

It was an island being born, molten at the center. Fine black sand rained down upon him.

An island . . .

George began to row hard back toward land. How long would it take? Another week or so to sputter out, to rise completely? So excited he saw nothing before him, not the blazing blue sky, not the smudge of clouds hanging behind the green hills, not the crowd of people on shore, not the boats being readied.

After a few weeks it might be cool; even fifty yards away the water had scalded. And then, how long before anything could grow? The ferns would be first, their ancient spores drifting . . . But how long before birds flew over, dropping seeds as always, oblivious? Fruit with wings, Mr. Clarence called them. The main things he'd bring himself. Barges of soil, lupine. Then the plants that prepare the soil, and as soon as he could, all he needed to live. He stopped rowing and turned back to look. Around the island hovered a steamy light, radiant against the blue sky.

As he reached shore and coasted in on a wave, the first of the boats there was shoved out to sea.

"Good God!" Mr. Furnell shouted over the water as he rowed. "How often can this happen? A new land born before our eyes! We'll have it! The Americans will have it, before the Portuguese. We'll have it before the British!"

And he disappeared beyond the swell of a wave, a flag fluttering after him.

14

*B*UT WITHIN A MONTH, the new island was gone. Bit by bit it crumbled away, and one day it slipped back into the sea, along with the flags that harpooned it.

SOON AFTER, George left Saint Michael. By that time almost all the groves were ruined, and the planters had at last learned why. A minute gray Coccus parasite had started it. But there was, they heard, in the south of Australia, where settlers were starting to clear, a species of ladybird that might eat this creature. Maybe she could save the last oranges. Maybe George would find her.

And then he'd come back. Or maybe he wouldn't. Maybe on that lonely, ancient continent, partly paradise but in larger part hell, he would at last find his habitat.

IT WAS 1836 when George sailed for South Australia. By then, across the sea to the east, Pedro—having battled for both an old empire and a new—had died of tuberculosis, a few months after restoring his daughter's crown. Miguel was in permanent exile. Across the sea in the other direction, a treaty had been signed, forcing the Seminoles out of Florida. And in Australia, Aborigines had killed a colonial plant hunter. All the same, the town of Adelaide was being laid out in the bush, so civilization kept advancing. The electric motor had just been invented, as had the revolver. The following year, Victoria would be Queen.

HMS Beagle, 1836

As GEORGE'S SHIP sailed south, it passed another ship heading back to England by way of the Azores, a small schooner. In the cramped cabin where he had suffered physical torments for the past few years but also moments of revelation, young Charles Darwin, with his high forehead and wispy sideburns, was adding notes to his diary.

He had sailed along the coasts of South America, walked its plains, and climbed its mountains; he had traveled across the Pacific to Australia. The great journey of his life would soon be over. After all the climbing, shooting, collecting, and pinning, he would be back in England, with his precious collections and—imagine—a fascinated *public* awaiting him. One last stop in this Portuguese archipelago. He gazed out his window at the nearing islands, green and peaked and wreathed in cloud. The great Captain Cook had stopped in sixty years earlier. Which, as he more than anyone knew, was a mere dot of time, but in *these* sixty years so much had changed . . . Sometimes he felt that though he followed Cook's watery trail, it was an utterly new world he was finding.

Darwin went back to his journal and turned to the pages about the Pacific archipelago that so impressed him, the Galápagos: volcanic islands newly risen, their black mineral surfaces still being draped with life. What he pondered above all, the extraordinary tortoises.

> *One was eating a Cactus & then quietly walked away. The other gave a deep & loud hiss & then drew back his head . . . Surrounded by the black Lava, the leafless shrubs & large Cacti, they appeared most old-fashioned ante-diluvian animals . . .*

He had tried to ride one but couldn't keep his balance and soon felt foolish astride the grand creature. They could get to be awfully old. He'd seen one with 1786 carved in its shell! They might be as old as trees. Yet within twenty years they would all be captured, overturned, scooped out, and eaten; not one would remain. Just as, he suspected, the kangaroos of Australia would soon be gone. Men did what they must to live, after all.

Darwin looked down at the page and tapped his pen against the table. The boat, as always, was rocking. Perhaps he's scratch out those sentences about none of the tortoises or kangaroos remaining. There was enough about extinction already. The poor absurd glyptodon, the lazy lost mylodon, of which he was so fond. Poor giant sloths, they had not been prepared for those northern predators, and certainly not for men: they were so slow and gentle that moss grew in their fur.

Yet that they *were* lost, like the terrible lizards, that nothing remained but bones, and that the bones could be found in the places he'd found them . . . Oh, it fascinated him, how it all fascinated him, the surface of this astonishing globe. The upheavals and changes of which it was capable!

Darwin looked up from his journal through the open cabin door, out at the drifting clouds, the rising and falling surface of water. He thought of his days in Chile and was grateful again that he, like Humboldt, had been granted an earthquake. He searched for the page.

> *The world, the very emblem of all that is solid, moves beneath our feet like a crust over a fluid; one second of time conveys to the mind a strange idea of insecurity . . .*

YES, THEY fascinated him, the awfully sublime movements of nature! And above all, the mystery of mysteries: how the possessors of that fragile thing called *life* appeared upon the mineral globe, how they became scattered across it.

The Amelia, 1836

November 14
Father having sold all and purchas'd blocks in a new province of Australia that is to be open & free, I, Sarah Ligith, commence this journal as we set sail from London Docks to record what no doubt will be the adventure of my life. The place is to be named for King Wm.'s queen, Adelaide . . .

December 3
We have been blessed with the trade-wind &, after a stop in the Azorean islands, have followed a course nearly direct. We are now only four degrees north of the Line and feel the

heat excessively. I have seen multitudes of flying fish, and porpoises, & three whales. When the sea is calm a number of albatross float at our stern, measuring nine ft. from wing to wing. To see such heavy bodies lift themselves into the air, I marvel and almost believe that we too might one day make the air our medium, and how I would wish to see that.

December 10
The heat has been so great that the unmarried men sleep upon deck at night & one must take care in the morning to stay clear of them. My own nightgown when I wake is as tho' dipped in a bucket of water. Others suffer swollen extremities—on deck I chanced upon a great brooding, shaggy fellow, sitting in a nest of bedding & struggling in silent despair to force his poor swollen feet into boots . . . Attempted to leaven the awkwardness of stumbling upon him thus by telling him what Doctor Forth assured me, that such swelling is a consequence of the extreme warmth and that one's blood-vessels become accustomed, and that in my case it is in hopes that the antipodean warmth shall mend my own fragile vessels that my family is emigrating . . . The fellow looked at me in purest horror & looked thus still as I hastened away.

March 2
Landed at last at Port River, with gratitude for what we recognize as an exceptionally fair passage. The port is scarcely a port, tho'—the men waded ashore through mud, we women perched upon their shoulders. G. Clarence (the swollen Brooder) conveyed me, my weight a bird's on his bulk and there being no one else to hand, as Father was well laden with Mama and Baby. All about us, long-awaited Terra Firma was no more than swamp and sandhills, & in such did we camp, with little but soft sand and rugs as our beds.

September 7

How can I convey what has transpired all this time, what we make of ourselves and this place? I cannot indeed—but shall try—it is a broad grassy land studded with stands of Eucalypts, the Torrens wandering through it, Red River gums growing all along, & yellow wattle, & flowering weeds whose names I do not know. In the hills around are peppermint trees and stringy-bark & this is what is used to make shingles to roof our cottages, which are of rammed earth and clay. Some have arranged to ship in ready-made houses of wood from home, but the white-ants shall take care of these, I do think. G.C. has been gathering stones for his own home and is putting in almond-trees and grape-vines and I do believe he shall have some success . . . Red kangaroos are to be seen, as expected, as well as white and black cockatoos, parakeets, magpie geese, and black swans flying far above, in pairs . . .

PART IV

CLOSE TORTOISE.

So HERE IT WAS, fifty years later than she'd planned, but Violet was traveling at last.

Not quite as she'd dreamt, though: to board a steamer at Port Adelaide and set sail into the world—those days were long gone. No, she would fly, and with a group. The flight from Adelaide to Sydney didn't leave until noon, but she'd been ready since last night. By eight in the morning she was waiting with her luggage on the veranda, wearing a hat that would crush if she packed it, and the green dress she'd designated her traveling dress, and sandals to avoid what she'd heard about swelling. George was to come at twenty past and take her to the airport.

"The big day at last, Mum!" he called out when he'd parked. He climbed from the Opel in a bright shirt, squinting. "All set?"

"All set." She looked at the door of the bluestone house for a moment, took a breath, and locked it. George rolled her suitcase to the car and helped her in. When he got in himself, he glanced at her with his close-set eyes.

"So off you go," he said, and patted her hand. "Merry old England."

Vi could feel her heart beating in her dress. She opened her purse to check the tickets again, and as George started the car she felt a clutch, as if she might never come back.

"It's only three months," she said.

But they looked at each other before pulling out, and it was clear they both saw Alf. Alf who had been gone only three months and would be gone, somehow, forever.

George drove through the leafy streets, out to the round-about, and on toward Glenelg, but all that time Violet kept seeing Alf, as if in leaving home she left him, too. Glimpses always flared when she did the washing up or sat in the lav or otherwise least expected him: an old man coming out to the garden in the sun, with his thin white legs, his shorts and argyle socks and loafers, his long face beneath a silly broad hat: how he squinted into the brightness but couldn't see her sitting in the shadow of the gum. How he sighed, sat a moment on the step, then rose and went back up to the veranda, reaching behind privately to pluck the shorts from his bum as he wandered back inside. This was how Violet saw him most often. Why this one image she couldn't say, of all the millions in her head. Not even millions, for that would mean they were separate, when really her visions of him were one long stream that had flowed fifty years. Perhaps this one because it was almost the last: Alf sighing and wandering away.

And oh it hurt her, not knowing *where*.

By the end he had lost an eye and wore a glass one, but right up until then—when he went walkabout one night all over the neighborhood, with just his pajamas and slippers and single good eye, poking an old hand into the darkness before him—right up until then he had been sturdy, he had known his way no matter what, no fear. Through the years of sheep and dippings and droughts, until finally, when they'd saved enough, they gave the works to George (who turned it over to alpacas, of all things) and bought the little bluestone villa in town.

But now Alf had been gone three months, and that was the true reason she was traveling. You ought to get *away,* they all said. Now's the time, Vi. Get out and see the world!

"You'll have a grand time, Mum," George said. He reached over and squeezed her wrist. "I know it."

She nodded. Of course she would; she was seeing the world. At Sydney airport she'd meet up with the group, and they'd fly to Singapore and then straight to London. Without even thinking, when she'd first looked into it with the travel agent, she knew she'd first go to London. There was no question; her blood pulled. From England to Paris, Munich, and Vienna, then on down to Venice and Rome, and that would take care of Europe; anyway, the agent said so. Then on to America, until the bit (after England) she looked forward to most: a "Paradise" cruise in the Caribbean. The maddening thing was that she wouldn't see Rosalind and Alice, but she'd had to rule out Asia, Africa, and the Middle East as just too much, too overwhelming. And anyway, they'd been back for the service.

On the flight from Adelaide to Sydney, Violet pressed her forehead to the oval of glass and stared down at the astonishing, rippling red earth. In Sydney the travelers were to meet at check-in. A big, pleasant-looking girl named Hazel stood in the middle of a mob of oldies, brandishing what appeared to be a shepherd's staff. And just as you'd think, the group was all women, except for one small fellow called Irv, who'd taught history. There was a Mary and an Eleanor and a dozen others, with walking sticks and hats and pink, sun-damaged faces. Links formed at once as they waited at the departure gate, and though Violet did her part (as always), she was now too distracted by the journey itself. She finally realized she was *going*. England in twenty-four hours! She did not think the word *home* but that's what it was like.

Qantas 50 began to board, and they flocked together, excited. Violet showed her passport and ticket and began walking in her green dress down the ramp, and it felt like a dream, as if she was being married or walking a plank, and at a turn in the ramp, when no one was near, she whispered, "Look Mum—I'm going at last."

She would have whispered to Alf as well, but surely he already knew.

ON THE LONG, long, merciless flight, Violet tried to sleep but couldn't. She moved her toes and poked her calves as Hazel had advised them. She smiled at the old girls in her group as they lurched through the aisles to and from the lav and clutched the backs of seats and chatted. The sun never rose, not once in twenty-four hours, and aside from Singapore, which went by in a daze, there was never anything to see each time she pushed up the blind but an illegible scattering of lights. Finally they flew above Europe—it *had* to be Europe, because it was dawn. But only cloud lay beneath them, there was nothing but whiteness.

"Not a glimmer!" cried someone from the other side of the plane, peering out her own window.

In the seat in front of Violet, Irv rose and swiveled his old neck like a turtle to address her. He was already such a pet among the women that Violet had decided to ignore him, and this had the usual effect.

"Not a glimmer of Europe!" he said, and made himself

look astonished. "Then perhaps it's been a hoax. Hmm? Perhaps there never was any Europe at all. Then where would the rest of us be, I ask you?"

Violet laughed, as did the others, although whether they got it wasn't clear. She fixed her gaze through the thick glass window and into the white blanket beneath them.

There was a sudden rip in the cloud and a glimpse of actual land, and she realized with shock that it was real, they were almost *there*. The plane plunged into whiteness, then broke through, and there it was, clear beneath them, merry old England, soft and green and raining, as everyone had wagered.

THE FIRST DAYS in London Violet kept up eagerly. She inspected the paintings in the National Gallery, admired the fountains and statues and churches and Tower, and nodded attentively as Hazel rattled on. She found herself sneaking glances at the Londoners hurrying by with shopping bags and satchels. As if she might recognize someone, as if there might be someone she *knew*. Not that she actually knew anyone to ring up and so forth, but there might be . . . something. In Harrods and at the British Museum and outside at Piccadilly Circus, she glanced around at all the faces, looking for a family resemblance, someone like herself or Alice or that first forebear with his big hands and stricken eyes. The group shuffled along with their sticks and umbrellas, and as they ordered tea Violet became aware of their accents. She became aware of the Londoners aware of their accents. Without going so far as to be ashamed, she began to speak more softly.

At first she made a game effort to keep track of where they went on the map and to note down everything they did, but soon the busy streets and circles were beyond her, and it put her off balance the way the sun (what there was of it) no longer hung where it used to. North and south, she could not keep them straight, and by the time she'd concentrated on the fact that if they were *facing* the sun at nine in the morning, then to her right was south, not north as usual, the group had already moved away from that spot and she lost her bearings all over again.

So Violet never quite knew where she was in London, and this, together with the damp and smog and chaos and motion, began to make her feel vague. She drew about her more snugly the blue wool cardigan she'd bought at a shop, and with a little gesture of abandonment she flung herself back in the coach seat, shoved off her shoes, and let the buildings, pub signs, raw faces, and wet trees pass by through the glass.

Gradually she had to admit, although only to herself in the hotel bed at night, as she stared up at the ceiling and all around was dark and foreign, that something was not right. It wasn't just staying in a hotel and riding in that coach and being on her feet so much; it wasn't the disorientation or even the slight surliness or would you say *disdain* of the shopkeepers and waitresses when this mob of Australians came in; it was something else, something worse: an ache.

As if she'd finally come home and nobody greeted her.

Or as if, after all the years of loyal imagining, there turned out to be no connection between this place and home.

AFTER TEN DAYS the group was done with London and made excursions out of town. There was more space and light, despite the heavy gray clouds. Light seemed to rise from the ground.

"So green!" they cried as they wiped condensation from the coach windows and peered out. "Have you ever in your life seen such green?"

"Greener in Ireland," said Mary, who had traveled more

than the rest. She sat in front of Violet and had a flawlessly smooth coif.

The bus stopped in gravel car-parks, and the ladies and their lone prince issued out: first was the famous Botanical Gardens at Kew. This soothed Violet, far more peaceful than London's crowded galleries and drowning streets. She wandered along the serpentine paths, between tall green hedges, into enclosures of flowers, past a Chinese folly, down sloping lawns. She went with the others to the exotic collections, the great Palm House with breadfruit and cycads, then the Temperate House full of plants from the Americas, Asia, Australia.

But it was strange to be there, in England, walking along the aisles between tree ferns, palms, jacaranda, and gums. She wandered over to some orange trees, and as she stood breathing the sweet white scent of the blossoms, she looked at the educational sign. It was good that they had such signs in these places, she always made a point of reading them, and she fished in her bag for her spectacles. This one was about citruses, the pests that plagued them, the predators that ate those pests. And who would have thought: the most famous predator was an Australian ladybird, found not far from Adelaide.

"Oh for goodness' sake," cried Eleanor from the other side of a fan palm, apparently reading another such sign. "Is *that* why a banksia's called that? Banks?"

"Didn't you know," said Mary.

Violet went to the other end of the glasshouse, stroking a soggy tree fern at a bend in the path. It was soothing to be near things from home, but unsettling. She felt both at home and oddly on display.

She went out the glass doors to the freshness and gray sky. What she wanted to see were bluebells, roses, great English oaks, things meant to be homely, but foreign.

And it was there, at Kew, outside the Palm House, as she

knelt in a meadow of bluebells, that she suddenly found herself in tears. For it seemed that somewhere in this English greenery was what she had yearned for, what she'd most missed.

But how could she miss something she did not even know?

As if in her heart she *belonged* to this place.

But how could you ever belong to a place? The claim was as airy as those mariners' lines drawn from the sea to the stars.

The others came out of the Temperate House, chatting, in their lavender dresses, yellow jumpers, and slacks.

"What are you doing there, Vi? In the violets?"

"They're not *violets*, Eleanor," said Mary. "They're bluebells."

"Come along, Violet. We're exploring the follies."

"But whatever's the matter? Violet! *Come* on."

And she did, of course, she blew her nose and got up and followed, but she only shook her head brightly when they asked what was wrong, for how could she possibly tell something so foolish?

As the group went along they stooped and inspected leaves and labels and made discoveries pertinent to their own gardens at home. They bought postcards and seed packets in the botanical shop, and Violet found a good card of an old monkey puzzle for Alice, and then they went to the Maids of Honour for tea and scones.

"But will it take, do you think?" asked Eleanor, studying the instructions on a packet of seeds.

"There's something very like it at the Botanic Gardens in Sydney, so I don't see why it shouldn't."

"They won't let those seeds in at home, you know," said Mary, as she returned from the ladies'. "Won't let you through immigration."

"What!"

"No seeds or plants may be brought in. Didn't you know?"

"Fancy not telling us before we bought all this loot!"

"Then I shall stuff it in my brassiere," declared Eleanor.

"Good girl," said Irv. "Close to your heart."

THEN THEY WERE finished with England, just like that. With almost a cry of disappointment Violet felt it spooling behind her as they crossed the Channel: merry England, brave Britannia, Britain whence they all had issued. And now it seemed that something that had never even been hers she had lost; she had lost forever her mooring.

AFTER THAT CAME Paris, more rain, more paintings, more churches and shops, the traffic on the wrong side of the road and the language adding to the bewilderment. So many things that people had made, such an awful lot of history. The coach sped along, and with the lights gleaming in the wet streets, it seemed to Violet that they floated in a stream. Then Munich, Salzburg, and Vienna, and over the Alps, during which even Irv clutched his armrest with marbled fingers as icy peaks rose against the sky. In sunny Venice, the group climbed over bridges and navigated passages and coped with all the painted Madonnas. Violet for one was overwhelmed. Then it was on to Rome.

Partway there the coach pulled over and parked in the middle of nowhere. There were dry stretching hills, fields of red poppies, a crow soaring in the sky.

"A treat," announced Hazel, her broad cheeks pink. "An Etruscan tomb that's rarely open, so we mustn't miss it."

The group squinted and followed as she led the way with her shepherdess staff over the dusty field. They clutched their sticks or one another's arms as she directed them down earthen steps into darkness.

When the lights came on, Violet blinked and looked around. The walls were covered with paintings, making it festive, for a tomb. The pictures on all sides were edged with painted tassels so that it seemed you were not underground but out in the open, beneath a tent set up for a wedding, and all the wedding guests lay around on couches, enjoying a feast. One picture struck her particularly: a man gazed right at her, holding up an egg between his forefinger and thumb. He looked as if he were showing her something everyone ought to know, a mystery they all should be in on.

What, the egg?

As if he would patiently present it, for thousands of years, to anyone who ventured into his tomb.

But why an egg?

She'd had one that morning for breakfast, soft-boiled, a special favor at the last pension. And for a silly moment, standing there in the tomb, she imagined that his egg, too, was soft-boiled. Of course not, it was surely fresh. But why an egg?

Then the light went off, and Hazel herded them toward the steps; time for the tomb keeper's lunch. But the egg and the painted Etruscan's eyes lingered before Violet as she groped her way up the crumbling steps in the dark, and it lingered still as the coach sped to Rome.

ROME WAS HOT and loud with Vespas, and it was clear at once that it would all be too much. The coach circled fallen marble columns and heaps of crumbling brick as Hazel told them of kingdoms, republics, and empires. And that only got them past Caesar! There was still the Vatican, the Renaissance, the hundreds of churches, and who could bear another bloody church?

When the coach stopped at the Pantheon and the flock

filed in, Violet slipped away to be alone. She went to the center of the great dim drum and stood still among the echoes
and shuffling feet. A ray of light slanted through the hole in
the dome, and she realized that the ray would travel very
slowly around the drum, like an inside sundial. She looked at
it slanting into the dimness. Now and then someone walked
through the light, so that once a child's curling gold hair and
then a woman's worried brown eyes were lit up like magic.
The very sight made her almost weep again. As if this slim
beam of light in the dimness *meant* something, and against
it all the buildings and cities and paintings and sculptures
did not amount to a thing.

"Too much traveling," she whispered. "You're in a state."

And that afternoon, in a catacomb, she fell to pieces. It
was a tunnel that ran through shelves of moldering bones,
bones so old they were crumbling back into earth. Violet
didn't mind the bones, really, and she didn't even mind the
closeness; it was just the thought of all those people. She suddenly realized, fully realized, that those bones had once been
people, making breakfast and walking in the grass; they had
lived as vividly as she did and imagined they were something.
Yet here they were, nothing left but names scratched in rock.

For how did it happen? *How* did it happen? When she
still remembered clear as a bell how flushed and quick she'd
felt in the riverbed, plunging her hands into Alf's thick hair!
She still could see his shocked eyes, the red crease from the
spectacles on his nose!

Where did all of it *go*?

It was too much. She turned and pushed her way out
through the others, through their fleshy old arms, their hair
and humid breath.

Out in the brightness, in the car-park, Violet fanned herself and tried to recover. She blinked and concentrated on

ordinary things: the square of dirt she was standing on, an umbrella pine, a man selling ice cream, plain ordinary things in the world.

But it didn't help. She stood there, an old freckled woman as slight as a bird, in a blue shift and sandals, staring down at the lonely, packed ground.

Irv was the first to emerge. He came out blinking like a mole, and when he saw her he shuddered dramatically.

"Enough old bones for me!" he cried. "Bad enough to have them knocking inside you."

"Oh don't I *know* it!" said Violet. "Don't I!" And overwhelmed with gratitude, she searched in her purse and flourished a handful of lire and treated them both to gelato.

BY THE MIDDLE OF September they were through with Europe and set off to America. There Violet did make a valiant effort. She struggled to follow why tea had been hurled into the harbor and what the proclamations of 1776 really came to, but as the coach drove on, and on and on, the things that stayed with her were the small ones: the bluebells, that ray of light, the Etruscan and his egg.

Sometimes she looked out the coach window in wonder, at the asphalt and glass and telephone wire and billboards, the world that people had made. How funny that it had turned out like this. Not that anything was so wrong with it. Just that it could have been anything else.

THEN FINALLY, after all the coach rides and hotels and early-bird dinners, it was time for Violet's cruise.

*T*HE *PARADISE* LEFT Miami at dusk. Violet's cabin was beneath the anchor, but she didn't notice that first exciting night as she stood with the others on deck, waved to a crowd she didn't know, and sang out, "Bon voyage!" Only later, as she dressed for dinner, was she shocked by the screech of the chain when the huge anchor was lifted from the sea floor.

But she didn't mind. To be at sea! To be on the *Paradise,* sailing the tropics! Now that she was finally sailing, she brought out the clothes she'd saved for the ship, as if they were a trousseau: white hat, blue-and-white blouse, floppy blue trousers, and a silk scarf she tied around her neck in what she felt was a jaunty sailor's knot.

Bahamas, Antigua, Barbuda, Barbados . . . Diligent once more, Violet went to the lounge on the upper deck, where a framed map showed everywhere they would sail. The names entranced her, so exotic and old, Spanish or Indian she wasn't sure, and she loved how the islands looked on the map: scattered out upon the emerald sea, like a little echo of the East Indies.

East Indies and West—only now did this occur to her, that there were both East and West Indies. So whoever named them had stood in between, because it was all a matter of where you stood, wasn't it?

"They shall be my East and West Indies," she recited aloud to the empty lounge, holding a hand out before her. She couldn't remember any more of the passage.

Bahamas, Antigua, Barbuda, Barbados. The names were entrancing, but worrying, too. Tropical and lush, full of sugar and bananas and mangoes and saffron, but with a sun much too bright, and violent.

THE HUGE *PARADISE* glided out to sea. From the main deck the water was so far down you could almost not notice it. Violet walked along the brilliant white deck until she found a stair that led to a lower deck, then another stair to a lower one still, until she reached the lowest. There she found a place where she could lean out and see and smell as much as possible.

So much light and distance after all those cities! The sea sparkled and glinted, hazing at the horizon into the blue sky. The Caribbean didn't smell like her own ocean; it was warmer and more fecund, more green; but still it bore a hint of those cold waters that used to crash upon her tripey rocks. She clung to the rail and breathed the sea air, felt the sun on her old cheeks, looked out beneath a shading hand. She grew dreamy, even dizzy, at the vastness of the sea and the open sky.

Surely, she thought, this was how it once was. Long ago, centuries ago, when we first set sail to discover new lands.

And even before that, well before that, before all these cities and ships had been made, before we even existed.

BAHAMAS, ANTIGUA, Barbuda, Barbados. The ship steamed through the blue waters, trailing a plume of smoke. When it reached its first port, Violet and Irv and Mary and the others put on their hats and clutched their cameras and purses and hurried down the gangway. Into the sun, into a stew of people clamoring with goods, into markets and shops.

"Genuine saffron!" cried Mary. "Actually *plucked* from crocuses. I'll certainly have some of that."

"Better stuff it in your brassiere," murmured Eleanor.

"A stamen is not a seed."

They toured the market and bought things, snapped photos of women with baskets of fruit, went off in a coach to the sugarcane fields.

It was gorgeous, blinding: banana plants with the sun shining through their huge flopping leaves, and bunches of unripe fruit; palm trees with clusters of coconuts dripping; yams and pineapples rotting in the dirt. It could not have been less like dusty Europe and seemed almost to simmer, alive. Violet looked through the tinted glass at it all whizzing by. There was something almost *primitive* about it, something about the abandoned palm trees with their explosion of fronds on the horizon and all the exuberant plants she could not even name, and the shocking intensity of the sky. Even the clouds seemed overlarge, as if they'd only just been born and were full of life and power. Paradise was what everyone called it, fruit falling into your hands. But it was sinister, too, she could feel it: a poison in the place's blood.

Today had been Saint Vincent. Where, Hazel told them, those famous breadfruit trees had finally been brought after causing so much trouble for Captain Bligh and the *Bounty*.

And hadn't the plantation workers rejoiced to see the trees unloaded.

Plantation workers! Violet glanced quickly at Mary and Irv. Even *she* knew more than to call them that. And she'd read somewhere they wouldn't even eat it.

THE SHIP STEAMED ON through the emerald waters, the decks blinding in the sun. It docked at one hot green island after another, and again and again Violet, Mary, Irv, and the others set off down the gangplank.

"Aren't you coming to the market?" said Mary. "*Come* on. We're all going."

But after a week Violet was truly through with shopping. More than two months of shopping on two different continents and half a dozen islands. She already had presents for Rosalind and everyone, an enormous bag of heaven knew what that nobody really needed. She waved Mary away with her hat, and while the others squinted and parceled out dollars to dark hands for little carved boxes of nutmeg and mace, she stood in the shade of a tree and looked on, fanning herself with a big leaf, uneasy.

When she and Mary walked back to the ship that evening, they were followed by a boy showing them beads, even though Mary had already bought a thing made of feathers. He had on a dirty T-shirt and no shoes, and his thin brown arms were draped with necklaces. He kept raising his hands and shaking them so that the beads jingled.

"No, no, thank you," said Violet, looking down at the boy and his dirty dark knees. She smiled and wagged her head *No*.

Still he kept waving and showing his beads, repeating words she could not understand.

"Truly," said Violet, "we're all done with shopping."

But now he circled them as they walked on, darting before them and dancing backward until he lost his footing and had to stop and then quickly circle them again, saying over and over words they couldn't understand, frantically shaking his beads.

"Now listen!" cried Mary. She halted and raised her hand, so that the boy flinched and let his arms drop.

"Wretched natives," she said, pulling Violet away.

But for an instant, before she turned and they hurried off, Violet saw in the boy's eyes a whole world pass through; she saw a little lost boy standing in the dirt.

WHEN THEY GOT BACK to the ship, Mary went to the lounge for tea, but Violet lingered on deck. She was troubled, she could not quite say how.

Well, *natives*, for instance. As Mary had put it. Yet was there a sole native left in the place?

Suddenly she couldn't follow the word. It didn't seem to have a meaning. *Native, native*, it meant where you were born. Yet also somehow *primitive*.

She gazed at the island as the boat blew its horn. That sound a lifetime ago had filled her with longing, down at the dock of Port Adelaide. Before Alf, and the sheep, and Rosalind and George and the alpacas and Alice, before she grew old, before everything. Below, the men in white uniforms slowly pulled back the metal gangways.

Captain Hook made the Lost Boys walk the gangplank; she remembered that from a picture. One boy after another was blindfolded and bravely set out on that plank over the sea, feeling his way with bare toes. She wasn't sure how it turned out. Had they dropped into the water? Or flown?

Now the men were throwing ropes, and the huge ship was unmoored. No one stood down on the dock, no one waved. Not that you should expect it.

A terrible thing once happened here. Mary had told them about it last night as they sat at the table over plates of pineapple and ham, sipping sweet wine. On this very island, she said, natives (*her* word) had massacred a flock of Americans at a roast-beef buffet in the golf club.

The little group was shocked. Violet murmured, too, but mostly she'd stared down at her plate and slid her pineapple back and forth. Because . . .

Well, there were crimes and *crimes,* she thought.

The boat was slowly moving away. Funny how little you felt it, up on deck. As if you weren't even on the sea. She gazed back at the island, its green hills and golf courses, its fields where bananas and sugar and breadfruit grew, and none of them were from there at all.

Had colonials really boiled Aborigines' skulls? And shipped them home as souvenirs?

The wind picked up, and she drew her blouse close, her scarf flitting at her neck.

She was tired.

The ship blew its horn again, and let out its long plume, and the island slowly slid away. But all she could see was that little boy with the beads, his marble eyes and dirty bare feet, that poor lost boy standing in the dirt.

THEIR LAST STOP before returning to Miami was the southernmost key of North America.

"What a relief," said Mary. "Civilization."

When the ship moored at the dock, the others trooped off as usual to the shops and bars, but Violet joined a group going to a seaside park.

To get to it they drove past tropical mansions half hidden in giant schefflera and palms bedecked with shiny red fruit, then past a barbed-wire military compound. Just when a wooded beach seemed unlikely, the road swerved, and before them lay a soft haze of green trees and the glittering sea. And who would have thought that the trees would be she-oaks—her very own casuarinas. A whole peaceful grove of them all the way from Australia: it seemed like a message from home.

Violet walked along a sandy path to a picnic table near a rock breakwater, where men stood fishing. She sat and looked out toward the blue water, as the she-oaks stirred around her. She plucked a needle like a strand of green hair and pulled it apart, segment by segment.

Huge clouds floated in the sky; a red propeller plane droned over. On the beach, a mustached man was taking pictures of his wife and baby. *"¡Allí! ¡Allí!"* he kept calling out, gesturing nearer the water, until the woman stood where he liked. The water drifted around her bare feet, and the light fell clear and lovely on her face and the smoky-haired baby in her arms.

Violet waited until the picture was snapped, then got up and wandered through the trees. Park rangers had posted an educational sign about sea turtles, so she stopped and put on her glasses. Photographs showed a big turtle planting her eggs in that very beach. First she swam ashore in the dark, then she crawled up to dry sand. She dug a hole with her flippers, positioned herself above it, and let down her curious shoot, and out rolled little round eggs, tumbling and glistening in the sandy hole. She covered them up, crawled back to the sea, and that was that, she swam away.

Just like planting, thought Violet. She'd forgotten that turtles laid eggs. Like birds—like dinosaurs even, once upon a time. She looked at the picture again, then turned and studied the empty beach. One day the baby turtles would hatch. Imagine sitting on that particular bit of sand when suddenly it started to shift and crumble, and out clambered tiny turtles.

She pictured them climbing from the hole, racing down to the waves, slipping into the drifting water. She could see them lose their footing, be pulled out to where the water was deep, tumble at first, then find they could swim, and paddle energetically with baby dinosaur flippers, set to sea.

Violet stood there, looking at the sand, at the waves.

Imagine all that life popping out of the sand. It seemed suddenly—a wonder.

Up the beach the others were calling. Time to go back to the ship, their last night. Violet hurried along the path to the coach.

DINNER THAT EVENING was melancholy. The last night of their travels! The group drank champagne and made brave toasts, but mouths turned down and cheeks trembled with efforts to shake away tears. Of course they'd be stuck together tomorrow for hours at the airport, and then for a bloody day and a half on the plane, but everyone knew by then it would be different. They'd already have taken their leave.

After dinner, Vi and the others went out on deck for the sunset. The ship sounded its mournful horn and let out its plume; coral clouds towered above wisps of gray, the sun slowly sinking. Violet took her place at the railing, while Mary and Eleanor and Irv and the rest sat on deck chairs. Everyone stared west, hoping one last time for the famous green flash that was supposed to come when the sun dropped in the sea but that so far, in two weeks, had never done so.

Irv had on his captain's cap and sat with his legs crossed, revealing glimpses of skinny white shank between the navy blue trouser cuffs and black socks. At dinner he had told them about something he'd just read in the paper, something that seemed to Violet to be all tied up with the journey. The huge egg of a Madagascan elephant bird, he said, had been found on the beach near Perth. A bird that had been extinct for a thousand years! All those years the poor egg, perhaps the last egg produced by the very last bird just before some fellow speared her, had bobbed about in the Indian Ocean, only now washing up on shore. "Imagine," Irv said, "stumbling upon something like *that* in the dunes."

And imagine, Violet had thought, how lonely it would be if it hatched.

The sun was nearly down. It touched the horizon, spilling gold in the water. They watched it melt until only a bright sliver remained. Then that too slipped into the sea and was gone.

They were quiet.

Mary said, "Well, that's that."

They shook their heads and pulled their wraps closer. Once the sun was down the air grew cool quickly, no twilight in the tropics. The color in the sky drained away.

Irv looked at the ladies to his left and right, gave a long whistling sigh, and placed his hands on his knees. "I am afraid," he said, "that the time has come."

"Irv!" they cried. "You're not going in *yet*."

He threw up his hands. "Much to be done before the morrow," he said. "Packing and all those postcards to write. Got a lot of American stamps."

He rose ceremoniously, turned to the ladies, and bowed. Then he went from one to the next, kissing each hand. "Good night, fair creatures," he said.

"Good night, sweet prince!" they chorused back.

Violet still stood a little way up the deck, and Irv now turned to her. He flung out his arm in salute, lifted his cap, and slowly swept it to his feet as he bowed. The ladies applauded; Violet blew him a kiss. Irv made a last dignified nod to the company and turned away. As he went down the darkening deck, he put one hand out to feel for the rail, and reached behind with the other privately to pluck the trousers from his bum.

Suddenly Violet fell to pieces. Irv, and lost Alf, and this last night of her journey, and everything seemed to be ending. She did not know what to do and turned away so the others wouldn't see, for what with the stirring smell of the water, and the thought of the sea turtle somewhere swimming, and the baby ones left behind, and that extinct egg bobbing alone for years, and all of her travels and all that she'd seen, everything overwhelmed her. It had to do with planting and hope, and being born, and being lost. So much wandering in the world! That's all it was, that's all it came down to. Out you popped in some spot and time, then you floated a few years, and that was that, good or wicked, down you went again. The promise or guilt or goodness or confusion, it all just went back under.

The ship steamed on. Violet clutched the rail, her silk scarf fluttering behind her.

In the darkening sky were darker clouds. In fact the sky roiled; the breeze was picking up. She blew her nose and pulled her cardigan closer.

The sea was growing rough—swells had been deepening so gradually she only now noticed how the ship rose and fell. When the dark swirling clouds began to spit, the others down the deck exclaimed and got up from their chairs. But Violet held on to her rail and watched the huge waves roll toward them.

"Vi!" called Mary. "We're going in."

But Violet wouldn't go, not yet. She waved Mary away and clutched the rail with both hands and stared out at her wind, her sea. Her thin cheeks were stung by the salt, and her hair blew and whipped at her face. The wind itself was now so strong it rushed through her, snatching her breath. She opened her mouth and shouted "Hoo hoo hoo!" but her voice was lost in the gusting. She was about to do it again when suddenly her scarf slipped from her neck and flew off, flew away with the wind. It soared up, against the dark sky, then down, flapping above the heaving water before it was sucked in.

And again, straight out of the blue—what a foolish time, but given the waves and the wind—again she thought, Ulysses! And the veil some sea creature gave him when his ship was smashed and he floundered in the water: a veil that was to save him.

But what did that mean? A flimsy, nothing veil? What in heaven's *name* could that mean!

The wind was a gale now. The ship heaved and rolled; rain slashed over the deck.

"Violet!" screamed Mary from the door. "Come in this instant! You are a *damned* fool!"

Violet did go then, her hair streamed in her eyes and her shoes slipped and skidded, while all around the wind tore up water and water swallowed the wind. She ran in behind Mary to the lounge, where the piano was sliding from side to side and plates and crockery were falling from tables and people had been thrown from chairs. She stumbled with the others downstairs, and suddenly she could not remember which deck her cabin was on. Mary shouted and pointed. Then she was on her hands and knees on the corridor carpet, her shoulders banging against the walls, and her head knocking once, but she got to her feet and crept sideways with her back pressed to the wall, until at last she reached her cabin, and who would think you'd still need your key!

But there it was in her purse like any other day, and she got inside and shoved the door shut, and then all she could do was fall upon the bed, cling to the mattress as it rose and fell, her eyes and mouth open at the pillow.

At some point she was so exhausted she climbed, in her wet clothes, under the covers, and slept. She dreamt of water. It sloshed at the porthole, until the glass dissolved and became water itself, because glass was liquid, wasn't it? Liquid sand. And water rushed in and rose all around as she lay in the bed, it streamed and sloshed and rose, and seeped into her mouth, flowed over her skin, until like glass she, too, dissolved, until at last she was no longer herself but water, and it was so easy.

3

THE NEXT MORNING Violet's carpet and curtains were drenched. But that was all: the boat was steady, the sun shining through the open porthole. She got out of bed, squelched over the carpet, and put her tongue to the curtain, but it didn't taste salty. Just rain had come in, then, not sea. Outside, the water was green and sparkling beneath the big sky, as if nothing had happened.

There was no crockery that day, though: all smashed. To the passengers who appeared for breakfast the stewards handed hard-boiled eggs from their pockets. Several windows in the dining room were broken, but that was it; the piano stood in its usual place.

All the same, it was an adventure at sea. This was what Violet told herself as she took her seat at the table and laid a napkin on her lap and then cracked a hard-boiled egg on her head, forgetting she was among people. She looked around quickly. But across the room at another table an old fellow did the same, knocking an egg against his hairless head as if it were the most natural way. They all did, everyone in the dining room, so that for a moment the only sound you heard was the delicate sound of eggs knocking on heads. Then they quietly peeled their eggs, and held them up at the tips of their fingers, looked at them with contentment, shut their eyes, and bit.

4

*T*HEN THERE WAS the long, long flight, even longer than the other flights had been. Miami to Los Angeles, Los Angeles to Sydney. Perpetual night again, but this time they flew over the other half of the globe, and over a brand-new ocean.

The plane began descending soon after dawn. The sun was rising behind them, Violet's familiar old sun, the whole curving expanse of ocean now lit and gleaming like metal. Then the sun pulled free from the horizon, and how gorgeous it was beyond the rosy new clouds, at the edge of the Pacific. It was positively gold. After an hour Australia came into view—new land in the middle of the sea. All that ocean, years of dark ocean, and then the edge of Australia, just like that, a steep cliffed edge of rocks glowing red, a continent sitting in water. And on top, who would think: a fine veil of green. Violet pressed her forehead to the glass and thought she'd never seen anything so glorious.

———

GEORGE MET HER at the Adelaide airport. "You must be half dead," he said, as he threw her bags in the boot.

"A little wobbly."

They drove along the wide avenues home, and Violet looked out at the familiar but suddenly strange city passing by. She still seemed to be rocking, and she clutched the door handle, and concentrated on not being sick.

"So, Mum?" said George, at a stoplight. "How *was* it?"

"I'll tell you all about it later," said Violet, all about her adventures at sea.

THEY REACHED THE leafy section, her little bluestone villa. It had a veranda wrapping around three sides, and a garden in the back, and *villa* was a most exaggerated word, for it had only two small bedrooms.

"I can't just *drop* you, Mum!" said George, but yes, Violet told him, he could, and once her bags were safely inside, she sent him home to his wife and alpacas.

After the Opel had turned the corner, she waited a moment on the veranda. She didn't want to go in, not yet.

Then, in the sitting room, she stood still, and put out her arms to see if the rocking would stop. It was dim.

The house felt uneasy; it smelled stale. Her fingertips touched at the space, but she didn't feel anything. It didn't seem like hers. She knew it hadn't been lived in for a time, it needed its windows opened and taps run to come back to life, but still . . .

She dropped her purse on the tea table, sat down on the sofa, and peered around.

But the house was empty, no Alf.

"You'll have to do better than this," she whispered.

She got up and began to do things. She rolled her big bag into the bedroom and opened the windows and unzipped the case and started to sort out clothes. Stockings, shoes, nighties: she pulled them from her case, opened the wardrobe and drawers, and put things where they belonged. She tossed most in a pile for the wash, which she could never do without thinking of her old copper from those days long ago, and the wooden stirring stick, the blocks of blue, and that little house built of limestone and mallee roots out in the bleached yellow paddock. Just as she could never use the lav without thinking of that old long-drop, and sprinkling the ashes down.

So long ago, so very long.

But it was *not* so very long ago in the grand scheme of things, was it? She had seen this now that she had traveled the world. The old days could be far, far older. They could go all the way back to Rome. They could go much farther back still, to before we even *were.* And even that was not very long ago. In the great grand scheme of things.

Violet stood still again, in her bedroom with all the objects that were so familiar, in the solitude that wasn't.

From nowhere came to her the thought of a young woman she never even knew, but had only pictured. The young woman with the piece of stone in her hand, pumice that had erupted from Mount Vesuvius and made its way to South Australia, all the way to this young woman as she sat in a chair in a trance. And when she held that piece of foamy stone and spoke, everyone in the room, for a moment, had traveled as far as one could go, traveled to a mineral time, before life, and after.

VIOLET LOOKED AROUND at her bedroom, at the heap of clothes on the floor. She didn't want to do the laundry. She didn't want to be in this next phase, not yet; she must fend it off another moment. She hurried down the hallway to the kitchen and out, out to the veranda, the garden.

After all the glare and flaxen grass of their farm, here she and Alf had made a shady place. They planned the whole thing at the kitchen table, then did it themselves, drawing winding paths with powdered chalk on the ground and then laying down the pebbles, planting each tree and shrub. They had kentia palms from Norfolk Island, a lemon tree, an orange, pittosporum, two banksias, a lily pilly, a jacaranda with a staghorn fern at the hip, and a fan palm that, when Alice was small, had been no larger than she was, but now stood far above Violet.

And in the center of the garden was the blue gum, the one she privately called her big fellow. It was now so tall that she had to lean as far back as her spine would let her and squint up to see its top, blue sky showing through the dangling leaves. The bark was smooth and mottled gray, like a whale, and the trunk was long and sinuous, creased at the waist where it bent.

Far up, where the trunk divided and the white branches stretched out, the long thin leaves were flitting. Always that wind, the air rushing upon itself, rushing through the branches like water. So urgent, a current that pulled you on, and where did it ever end? With her eyes still full of her travels, Violet wondered again about that big man, that first George. Who really was he? Had he wanted to come? Was he some poor criminal like the others? And how had it been for him, blundering among the tree ferns and gums like a baffled animal, so far from home? And Alice when she was small, at the Adelaide airport about to fly away forever. Violet could still feel the hot wind of the engines and the sting in her eyes as they stood on the tarmac and she pressed something into Alice's arms. Because otherwise she'd forget. She'd forget where she was from! For how could you remember if you kept wandering on? Everything, the whole past, drifted off behind you, it fell away and sank and was gone, like all those poor souls whose bones lay in the ground, and Alf, among the deep roots . . .

Lost!

As if the word were cried by the wind itself, stripping.

Oh, but *lost* did not mean anything. What could it mean? Lost from *where*?

VIOLET STOOD STILL and took a breath.

As soon as she'd had a decent sleep she'd sort out the time zones and ring up Rosalind, tell her about her adventures, tell her everything she'd seen.

And she'd tell George to drive back tomorrow. She'd make—she'd make a pavlova.

She straightened her back, and looked up at the tree. Once she could put her arms right around it. She touched the crease in the trunk where it had bent after so many years in the wind, and with her other arm she tried to reach around, her cheek against the cool mottled skin.

Then, shy, she drew away. Strips of bark were lying around the tree's roots and all over the paving stones. She went to the shed to look for a rake.

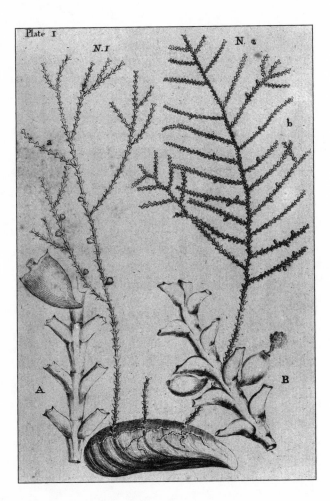

PART V

Scotland, 1981

THEY HAD TAKEN the ferry from Arisaig that morning and
now Alice and Lucy reached the little humped island they'd
been staring at from the window of their B&B. It was almost
September, almost time to head home. Classes would be starting soon. They'd come by train from Glasgow up to Arisaig
because they'd liked the sound of the *Road to the Isles*. And then
they'd decided to take the boat west to this island because Alice
wanted to see if there really were palm trees, as the guidebook
said, and Lucy wanted to hear the famous Singing Sands.

"They're the voices of souls lost at sea," Lucy said, as they
climbed the steep path from the ferry dock.

"It's just quartz," said Alice. "Underfoot."

THEY HIKED UP the hump in the middle of the island, past
low lush trees amongst which, sure enough, were cabbage

palms, so strange and tropical on this northern island. At the top of the bluff, where the path stopped, they could see the other coast, curving toward the Atlantic. It was so green there, slippery grass wetting their ankles as they walked down through meadows, the earth sinking soft beneath their boots. The sky seemed like gray marble in motion. It was hard to believe that the island had once been packed with cottages, crofters, and sheep, but the guidebook said there'd been thousands of people. Now there weren't even any stones left from the houses, no walls, no fence posts, nothing. As if the island had just shrugged everything off, and you'd never know anyone had been there. Rosalind would call her perverse, but Alice liked how the green of the meadows and bluff had closed smoothly over, like water. It made the place fresh and new, made it seem hopeful all over again.

When they came down the bluff to the sea, the grass gave way to white dunes and then a wide sweep of clean sand. It was spread out smooth, ruffed just a little by the breeze. There were no footprints, only birds' feathery tracks and the wriggling trails that crabs make. It was all coldly fresh, the grains of sand mineral and precise, as if they'd only just been ground from stone.

A chain of big black rocks ran along one edge of the beach, and seaweed lay strewn at the waterline. It smelled but Alice and Lucy dropped their packs by the rocks, took off their boots, and ran into it. They kicked through the seaweed, kicked it up like fallen leaves, jumped on the pods until they squirted.

Back by the rocks they ate their sandwiches, cheddar cheese on soda bread, apples bruised in shipping from somewhere else. Lucy got up and brushed off her hands.

"Got to pee," she said, and went off into the dunes. She liked to go very far away.

Alice sat for a while watching the waves, looking all along the horizon, just the gray sea, the bluff. She got her postcards out of the pack. One for Rosalind, one for Vi. Both had pictures of palm trees from this very island, and now at least she'd seen them and knew it was true.

Hi Grandmum! she wrote. It always felt funny to say that, it seemed affected since she was hardly Australian, but still that's what Vi liked to be called. *So now I'm in Scotland, up in the Hebrides. Windy and cool but would you believe palm trees actually grow here? Because of the Gulf Stream, they say. We took the ferry this morning—and guess what: I finally saw a whale. Wasn't even trying.*

There had been only six people on the boat from Arisaig, everyone in a slicker on deck and staring out at the water. The captain's assistant had made them tea, and Alice was sitting on a painted bench near the rail with the hot cardboard cup clamped between her knees. The sea rolled in big slow swells and it was a little bit sickening. Lucy was standing beside Alice in her hooded raincoat, looking over Alice's head out to the horizon, while Alice stared the other way. Suddenly Lucy's tea spilled on Alice's leg and she said, "Jesus God." From behind, in the water, Alice heard a sputtering sigh, and she turned just in time to see a smooth glossy back glide by underwater, a glimpse of its pleated tail.

"But did you see it?" said Lucy. They both stared at where the whale had gone under and then looked around hectically for where it might come back up.

"Minke," the tea-man said, coming back around with the pot. He'd looked pleased, as though the whale appeared regularly just for him.

So! Alice wrote. *Finally. Although I wish I'd seen its eye.*

She finished her postcards and put them back in the pack, but Lucy was nowhere in sight. The sky was clearing, all that marble drifting off, and blue showing through, sun warming her bare calves. She got up and climbed the black rock, cool and gritty under her feet, and stood a moment, surveying. Then she went from it to the next, climbed or jumped on them one by one toward the water, clinging with toes and hands. On the lowest rock near where the waves were breaking was a clear little tidal pool. She crouched down to study it.

Lucy appeared on a dune up the beach. She stood like an explorer, cupping her hands around her eyes as if they were binoculars.

"Find something?" she shouted.

Alice shrugged. "Shells."

But it was suddenly so amazing: one small pool in a hollow in this rock, water the depth of her hand, and in it lay hundreds of tiny shells. A miniature conch, black mussels the size of her fingernail, an orange crab as big as an ant drifting along the bottom. A whole little world. She looked up again at the seascape all around, rolling water, blowing sky, dunes, the green bluff rising behind; she looked in the way you look when what you really want is to *have* it, to absorb, but all you can do is take deep breaths of air.

But maybe you actually *did* absorb it. Maybe, if you looked hard and loved it a little, it did slip inside you, get transformed somehow, and you really did have it, you'd walk around with it forever. This little pool, like that water in Ecuador they weren't supposed to drink: that's what it suddenly felt like. Tiny transparent images of that mountain, the inky sky, and Vi's garden with the palm tree, all of it swimming inside her.

Lucy RAN DOWN the dune and then along the beach until she dropped to the sand and lay flat. She looked like seaweed, or a crumpled bird. After a minute Alice climbed from the rocks and went over; with bare ankles she could feel the fine grains of sand blowing. Lucy was lying with her ear pressed to the ground, and Alice stood over her and watched her listening.

"Aren't you probably supposed to hear the souls singing from up here?"

Lucy kicked for her to be quiet.

But if you crouched, stayed still, and held your breath, you could hear tiny grains of sand dancing along the surface. There was a pale haze at the water's edge where all those grains moved like cloud, and Alice listened to the breeze, the air itself, flowing. Lucy put a hand over the ear that was up.

"All right," said Alice. She lay down, too, put a hand over her ear, and shut her eyes. It was different now: deep secret grindings, the weight of the waves, your own heart and thin random breath. Suddenly she felt herself lying there, so small, and all those depths beneath and blue depths above. How Rosalind and the other women on the beach looked once, how little, when there was so much grinding beneath them, how nothing.

But what else?

She looked over at Lucy, whose eyes were shut tight, a strand of dirty red hair on her cheek. Alice held her breath again and listened hard. But there really was nothing you could call singing. She opened her eyes and rubbed her palm over the cool sand, making it squeak.

Lucy's eyes opened. "Do you even believe in souls anyway?" she asked.

Alice shook her head slowly, so that each ear touched the sand once.

Lucy sighed and rolled over. "Guess I can't, either."

Alice rubbed her bare feet over the sand until it almost

hummed. "But maybe you don't need to believe," she said. "Maybe it isn't necessary."

She raised her arms slowly and spread them wide, taking in the raw blue sky, the clouds, the tip of green bluff behind them. She looked at Lucy. Then she began singing softly: *"Satellite's gone up to the skies . . ."*

"Oh no," said Lucy. She covered her eyes. "Not again."

After a moment she stood up. She glared down at Alice and then raised her arms to either side, the black coat hanging like tired wings. She turned and stepped away. Gradually, with her arms outstretched, she began gliding, flying, moving in a big slow circle around Alice, navigating the wind currents.

"Satellite's gone," she sang, *"up to the skies . . ."*

Then Alice got up, too, and stretched out her arms, and began flying slowly around Lucy. For a while the two girls glided, making big figure eights on the sand.

ACKNOWLEDGMENTS

$\mathcal{M}$ANY PEOPLE HAVE helped me produce this book. Those I'd like most to thank are Alison Kahn, Duncan Campbell, John Shumate, Fernando Cruz Villalba, Juan David Morgan, Joyce Rischbieth, Nancy Robertson, James and Sally McGunnigle, Sally Rischbieth, Andrew Marsh, Pilar Alliende, and Catherine Cox, who have (not always knowingly) offered information, images, or houses, without which this would have been very different.

Crucial to the Australia sections have been the personal accounts, graciously shared, of my great aunt Jean Hensley; the memoirs of my grandmother Edna Hitchcox, grandfather Archibald Campbell, and great-grandfather Richmond Thomas Hitchcox; letters of my great-great-uncle Henry Clarke; and a history of the Hitchcox family by Josephine Prescott and Robert Brown.

Eighteenth- and nineteenth-century accounts of the Azores were invaluable, in particular those of Francis Masson,

Thomas Ashe, Captain Edward Boid, John W. Webster, Joseph Bullar, Robert Steele, Walter Frederick Walker, M. Borges de F. Henriques, and Frederick du Cane Godman. I've also drawn from Charles Darwin's *Diary of the Voyage of H. M. S. "Beagle"* (which Mr. Clarence is "reading" as it is written) and from Alexander von Humboldt's *Personal Narrative of a Journey to the Equinoctial Regions of the New Continent,* translated by Jason Wilson.

A version of the Ecuador section was first drafted while I attended Columbia University under an anonymous fellowship, so my thanks to all those at Columbia who offered suggestions and to that unknown sponsor. A much later version was written during a residency at the Rowohlt Foundation's Chateau Lavigny, for which I am grateful.

Finally, for their belief, perseverance, and particular ways of seeing, my gratitude once again to Becky Saletan and Geri Thoma. And, as always, for endurance, travel, and more, my love and thanks to Alex Wall.

PICTURE CREDITS

I. *Humboldt's Distribution of Plants in Equinoctial America, According to Elevation above the Level of the Sea.* Alexander von Humboldt, et al. Published by A. & C. Black, Edinburgh, 1851. Courtesy Khai Nguyen, King Ambler.

II. *Banksia serrata.* Watercolor by J. F. Miller, from a drawing by Sydney Parkinson made during Cook's first voyage, 1768–1771. Copyright The Natural History Museum, London. Reference: V7326/R.

III. *Tree-fern.* D. J. Ashworth, 1840s? Courtesy Alexander Turnbull Library, Wellington, New Zealand. Reference: A-209-001.

IV. *A Tortoise.* Stalker, ca. 1801. Courtesy Wellcome Library, London. Reference: V0022475.

V. *Sea Tamarisk. A vesiculated Coralline.* John Ellis, 1755. Courtesy Wellcome Library, London. Reference: M0010803.